The Cathy Chronicles

Books in the Sheed Andrews and McMeel Treasury Series

The Family Circus Treasury by Bil Keane

The Ziggy Treasury by Tom Wilson

The Momma Treasury by Mell Lazarus

The Marmaduke Treasury by Brad Anderson

The Tank McNamara Chronicles by Jeff Millar and Bill Hinds

The Cathy Chronicles by Cathy Guisewite

The Cathy Chronicles

by Cathy Guisewite

Sheed Andrews and McMeel, Inc.
Subsidiary of Universal Press Syndicate
Kansas City

ISBN: 0-8362-1115-4 cloth
      0-8362-1116-2 paper
Library of Congress Catalog Card Number: 78-70403

To mom and dad,
who made both
cathys possible.

This is Andrea, an uncompromising feminist and Cathy's best friend.

This is Irving, an uncompromising chauvinist pig and Cathy's boyfriend.

This is Emerson, an unsuccessful suitor.

This is Mom, Cathy's mom.

introduction

y parents are the kind of people who go around telling you to be grateful for everything that goes wrong in your life. Every big crisis has a purpose, they say. Every little disappointment, a bright and wonderful side.

Having grown up being forced to look for the good side of the worst moments of my life, I found that *Cathy* came about in a very natural way.

Instead of wallowing in the misery of waiting for phone calls that never came a few years ago, I was compelled to draw a picture of me waiting. . . .

Instead of agonizing over where love had gone, I couldn't resist putting my questions down on paper. . . .

And when I was filled with the drive to make radical changes in the way I was living, I couldn't help visualizing my determination. . . .

Although I never suspected I was creating a comic strip, *Cathy's* beginnings were in drawings just like these. They became a great release for my frustrations, and by sending them home, I discovered a great way to let my family know how I was doing without writing letters.

Anxious to have me do even better, my parents researched comic strip syndicates, sought advice from Tom Wilson, the creator of *Ziggy*, and, finally, threatened to send my work to Universal Press Syndicate if I didn't.

Just as Cathy began as a kind of self-therapy for my problems, she continues to be a voice for the questions I can never quite answer, and the things I can never quite say. Because our lives are linked so closely, she's affected by almost everyone I know and everything I do.

The strips in this book are arranged pretty much in the order that they first appeared in the newspaper. No doubt you'll notice that Cathy looks a little different toward the end of the book than she does in the first pages. But you'll also see a difference in her attitudes and relationships that are simply a reflection of the fact that in the last two years, I've changed too.

In this way, I want to always keep Cathy very real to life. Through her, I've learned that my little daily struggles are a lot like everyone' else's little daily struggles. The feelings I always thought that only I had are ones that everyone shares. But maybe just as important, writing Cathy has taught me one of the even greater lessons of life: anything is possible if you listen to your mother.

FRANKLY, CATHY, WE'VE NEVER HAD A WOMAN IN CHARGE OF TESTING HOUSEHOLD PRODUCTS BEFORE.

BUT MAYBE A WOMAN COULD HELP US JUDGE WHICH FLOOR WAX REALLY WAXES... WHICH MOP REALLY MOPS...

...WHICH ANT KILLER REALLY KILLS... ..WHICH...

THE GOVERNMENT'S BEEN AFTER YOU, HASN'T IT?

PLEASE WORK FOR US, CATHY!

ONLY IF YOU PROMISE TO READ MY RESUME.

OKAY, CATHY. YOUR FIRST ASSIGNMENT IS TO GET A SAMPLE OF WOMEN'S REACTIONS TO A PRODUCT CALLED "PRESTO WHITE".

YAAK! THAT'S THE STUFF THAT TURNED MY UNDERWEAR PURPLE!!!

THE KEY TO THIS JOB, CATHY, IS AN OPEN MIND.

THE TRICK, CATHY, IS TO DISCOVER WHICH MORE WOMEN PREFER-- "PRESTO WHITE" OR "NEW IMPROVED PRESTO WHITE".

THE OLD STUFF TURNED MY UNDERWEAR PURPLE... WHAT'S "NEW AND IMPROVED" ABOUT IT?

WE CHANGED THE NAME ON THE BOX.

...I WAS AFRAID OF THAT...

THEY WROTE "NEW AND IMPROVED" ON A BOX OF SOAP THAT TURNS UNDERWEAR PURPLE... AND THEY THINK PEOPLE WILL LIKE IT BETTER. THAT'S INCREDIBLE.

HI. I'M CATHY, FROM PRODUCT TESTING, INC. WHICH SAMPLE OF "PRESTO WHITE" DID YOU PREFER?

NEW AND IMPROVED!

THAT'S INCREDIBLE.

MY GIRLFRIEND, ANDREA, SAYS SANTA CLAUS IS A WOMAN.

MY BOYFRIEND, IRVING, REFUSES TO KISS ME UNDER THE MISTLETOE.

THERE'S ONLY ONE RATIONAL THING TO DO IN A SITUATION LIKE THIS.

EAT UP ALL THE CHRISTMAS COOKIES!!!

ANDREA! IRVING **HAS** DISCOVERED ROMANCE! HE PRACTICALLY **TOLD** ME HE GOT ME A SEXY NIGHTGOWN FOR CHRISTMAS!!!

OOH BOY--HE SAID IT'S SHORT, YELLOW, SEE-THRU AND LOTS OF FUN!!!

WHAT **IS** IT, CATHY??

...A PAIR OF DONALD DUCK BINOCULARS...

I DON'T KNOW WHAT'S WRONG, FLUFFY. BUT I DON'T FEEL ALL THAT GREAT ABOUT CHRISTMAS THIS YEAR.

I GOT NICE PRESENTS AND STUFF...BUT SOMETHING JUST ISN'T HERE ANYMORE.

MOM AND DAD!!!

SOMETIMES THE BEST CHRISTMAS PRESENT IS REMEMBERING WHAT YOU'VE ALREADY GOT.

CATHY_ YOU'VE GOT TO STOP WALLOWING IN THIS SELF-PITY. IT'S TIME YOU DISCOVERED YOURSELF.

DISCOVERED MYSELF?

I'M TAKING YOU TO A TRANSCENDENTAL MEDITATION CLASS TONIGHT.

DISCOVER MYSELF??

CATHY_ IT CAN REALLY PUT YOU IN TOUCH WITH WHO YOU ARE!!!

WHAT'S TO DISCOVER?

27

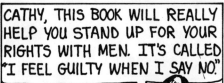

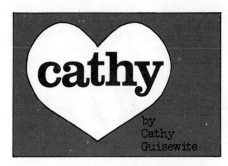

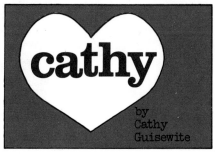

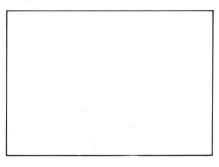

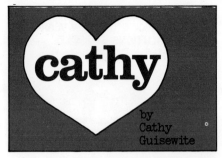

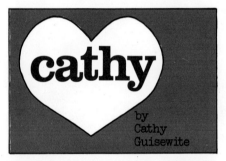

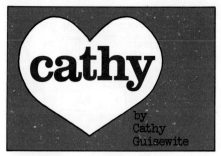

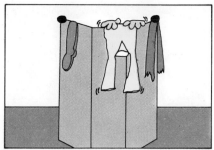

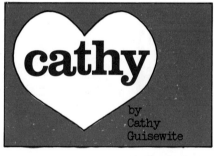

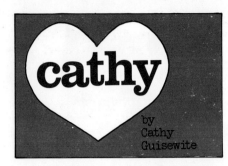

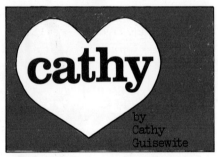

LOOK WHAT JUST CAME IN THE MAIL, ANDREA. THE "SKI 'N' SNUGGLE VAIL VACATION PLAN."

DO YOU THINK IT'S ONE OF THOSE DUMB SWINGER THINGS FOR DESPERATE SINGLES?

GOOD GOING, CATHY! YOU'RE FINALLY RECOGNIZING THE CHAUVINISTIC TRAPS DESIGNED TO STRIP A WOMAN OF HER DIGNITY AND MONEY !!!

BETTER HELP ME START PACKING, ANDREA.

ACTUALLY, CATHY THIS "SKI 'N' SNUGGLE VAIL VACATION" MIGHT HELP FREE YOU FROM THAT CHAUVINIST PIG, IRVING! YOU'LL BE INDEPENDENT! ON YOUR OWN !!

BREAKING AWAY FROM THESE MISERABLE LITTLE DEPENDENCIES IS SUCH A BIG STEP FOR A WOMAN !!!!

WHAT ARE YOU DOING ???

PACKING "FLUFFY"

WELL... IT'S A LITTLE STEP...

DEAR MOM AND DAD, WELL--HERE I AM ON MY "SKI 'N' SNUGGLE VAIL VACATION."

THERE MUST BE A MILLION GORGEOUS, SINGLE GUYS HERE !

THEY'RE ALL HOLDING HANDS WITH A MILLION-AND-A-HALF GORGEOUS, SINGLE GIRLS.

THREE MORE CUTE GUYS JUST WAVED AT ME ! MAYBE THIS SKI TRIP IS REALLY BRINGING ME OUT OF MY SHELL !!

MAYBE ALL THIS FRESH AIR AND EXERCISE IS REALLY DOING SOMETHING FOR ME !!!

MAYBE NO ONE CAN TELL WHAT I REALLY LOOK LIKE WITH ALL THIS SKI STUFF ON.

LOOK, ANDREA! I GOT VALENTINE'S DAY FLOWERS...AND I JUST **KNOW** THEY'RE NOT FROM MY MOM THIS YEAR!

OH, ANDREA! IRVING HAS FINALLY DECIDED TO BE THE SWEET, ROMANTIC MAN I ALWAYS DREAM HE IS!! **OH IRVING!!!**

CATHY ???

THEY'RE FROM MY DAD.

I AM WOMAN! I WILL NOT SCRUB FLOORS!!

I AM INVINCIBLE! I WILL OPEN MY OWN DOORS!!!

HEY, SWEETIE, WOULD'YA GET ME A BEER?

I AM SWEETIE. I'LL DO ANY STUPID LITTLE THING HE WANTS ME TO.

HEY, ANDREA, I'VE GOT A QUESTION. HOW COME YOU LOOK SEXY, STYLISH, HIP, PROGRESSIVE, AND SKINNY WHEN YOU STUFF YOUR JEANS IN YOUR BOOTS...

...AND WHEN I DO IT, IT LOOKS LIKE I'M WALKING ON TWO HOT DOGS?

HOW DO YOU **KNOW**, ANDREA? HOW DO YOU **KNOW** IF A GUY IS GOOD OR BAD FOR YOU?

JUST LISTEN TO YOUR FEELINGS, CATHY. YOU CAN TELL IF A RELATIONSHIP IS GOOD AND FAIR IF YOU JUST ASK YOUR CONSCIENCE.

HELLO, MOM?

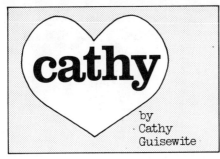

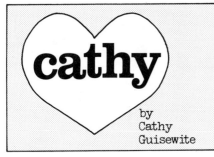

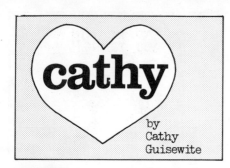

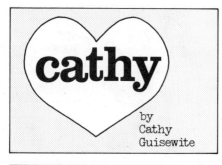

I hate being on a diet so much that I have never managed to stay on one for more than twenty minutes. Which probably best explains why it took me a full six years to lose forty pounds. And why Cathy struggles almost weekly with her weight.

She is constantly looking for the miracle diet plan that will not only dissolve pounds and inches without exercise, starvation, or inconvenience . . . . but will do it all before tonight's 7:30 date.

As Cathy would be quick to tell you, when you're overweight, you don't have *time* to lose weight. You're waiting for a transformation you believe will change every part of your life for the better.

Still, it isn't quite as simple as feeling all her problems would be solved if she were thin, and then eating to solve all her problems. When you're obsessed with food for long enough, food becomes a drive all its own. Something that no one who hasn't eaten a hot fudge sundae while hiding in the closet can begin to understand.

Learning to laugh at my failures instead of torturing myself for them helped me lose weight more than any diet ever did. I'm not suggesting that reading Cathy, and laughing along with her dieting problems, is any new miracle weight-loss plan. But she can offer some comfort; some understanding; and even if you're not losing weight, a few moments when you don't have to feel so miserable about it.

Unfortunately for all of us, it *is* possible to laugh and stuff yourself with Twinkies at the same time. Believe me, I've done that, too.

WHAT ARE YOU DOING DRINKING A CUP OF COFFEE, CATHY?!

DON'T YOU REALIZE THERE'S A COFFEE BOYCOTT GOING ON?!!

DON'T YOU SEE THAT PRICES WILL NEVER GO DOWN UNLESS WE ALL WAKE UP TO OUR RESPONSIBILITIES AND DEMAND CHANGE?!?!

HOW AM I SUPPOSED TO WAKE UP WITHOUT A CUP OF COFFEE?!!!

THE COFFEE BOYCOTT IS MORE THAN JUST A CHANCE TO FIGHT THE INJUSTICES OF HIGH PRICES, CATHY.

IT'S A CHANCE TO PROVE HOW **DYNAMIC** WOMEN REALLY ARE! THAT WE ARE **NOT** LAZY AND PASSIVE! WE WILL NOT LIE BACK AND LET THIS HAPPEN!!!

WHAT DO YOU REALLY **NEED** COFFEE FOR, ANYWAY, CATHY?!

TO BRIBE MYSELF OUT OF BED.

WHAT AN OPPORTUNITY WE'VE GOT IN THIS COFFEE BOYCOTT, CATHY! I MEAN, IF **WOMEN** QUIT DRINKING COFFEE, IT'S ONE THING.

BUT IF EVERY SINGLE SECRETARY AND WIFE IN AMERICA **REFUSED** TO SERVE HER BOSS OR HUSBAND A CUP OF COFFEE--**JUST THINK WHAT WE'D HAVE**!!!

A HIGHER NATIONAL UNEMPLOYMENT AND DIVORCE RATE.

HI, CATHY. WHAT ARE YOU UP TO?

I'M JUST DOING WHAT EVERY NORMAL, HEALTHY, SINGLE AMERICAN GIRL DOES TO GET READY FOR SATURDAY NIGHT, MOM.

I WASHED MY HAIR, STRAIGHTENED UP THE APARTMENT, PUT SOMETHING REAL COMFORTABLE ON...

YOU HAVE A BIG DATE TONIGHT??

I'M GETTING READY TO WATCH 'MARY TYLER MOORE.'

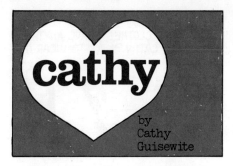

"HOW TO FIGURE OUT IF YOU'RE TOO FAT"...

HEY, ANDREA!!

LOOK, ANDREA! I CAN QUIT MY DIET!! THIS CHART SAYS I'M AT MY IDEAL WEIGHT!!!

I THINK YOU DID IT WRONG, CATHY.

SEE, YOU'RE SUPPOSED TO FIGURE HEIGHT WITH YOUR SHOES OFF, NOT ON.

YOU DO NOT HAVE A LARGE FRAME-- YOU HAVE A SMALL FRAME.

AND YOU HAVE TO SUBTRACT TWO POUNDS FROM YOUR IDEAL WEIGHT FOR EVERY YEAR YOU'RE UNDER 30.

I JUST BECAME 29 POUNDS OVERWEIGHT IN THREE MINUTES.

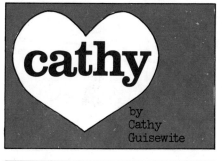

HI ANDREA. IT'S CATHY.

I'M REAL SORRY IF I WOKE YOU UP, BUT I'VE BEEN THINKING ABOUT WHAT YOU SAID...

JUST LET ME SEE IF I HAVE THIS STRAIGHT, ANDREA. IF I BECOME A HOUSEWIFE AND COOK MEALS, I'LL BE A SUBSERVIENT SLAVE...

...BUT IF I WERE A CHEF IN A RESTAURANT, I'D BRING DIGNITY TO ALL OF WOMANHOOD.

IF I SPEND MY DAYS CLEANING BATHTUBS AND TOILETS, MY STATUS AS A FEMALE IS EQUAL TO A GROVELING WORM...

...BUT IF I GO TO WORK FOR THE SEWER COMPANY, I'LL MAKE HEADLINES AS A FEMINIST STAR.

WHAT'S THE DIFFERENCE, ANDREA?! WHAT MAKES THE SAME MEASLY JOB AN INSULT IF YOU DO IT AT HOME, BUT AN HONOR IF YOU MAKE IT A CAREER?!!?

MONEY.

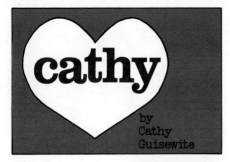

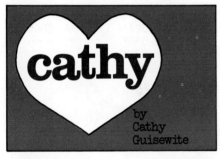

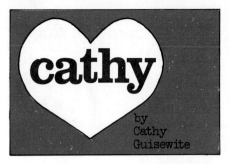

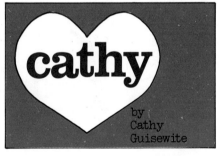

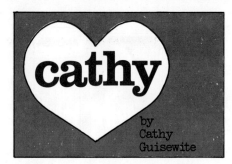

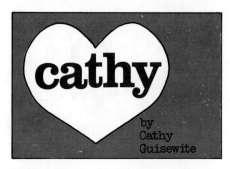

JUST ONE MORE GAME, CATHY!

FORGET IT, IRVING. I'M SICK OF PLAYING TV TENNIS.

IN FACT, I'M GETTING A LITTLE SICK OF **ALWAYS** DOING EVERYTHING YOU WANT **!! IN FACT, I...**

...IRVING ???

IRVING HAS BEEN HYPNOTIZED BY A TV TENNIS GAME.

IRVING, SNAP OUT OF IT !!

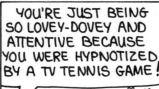

YOU'RE JUST BEING SO LOVEY-DOVEY AND ATTENTIVE BECAUSE YOU WERE HYPNOTIZED BY A TV TENNIS GAME !

YOU'RE SUPPOSED TO BE ALOOF AND PIGHEADED !! INSULT ME OR SOMETHING, IRVING!

WAIT A MINUTE.

OH, IRVING. EVER SINCE YOU WERE HYPNOTIZED BY YOUR TV TENNIS GAME, YOU'VE BEEN SO NICE I CAN'T STAND IT.

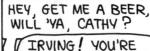

HEY, GET ME A BEER, WILL 'YA, CATHY ?

IRVING ! YOU'RE WELL !! **YOU'RE BACK TO NORMAL !!!**

AND WHILE YOU'RE IN THERE, HOW ABOUT A COUPLE SALAMI SANDWICHES.. AND A....

TENNIS ANYONE ?

CATHY, ARE YOU STILL BEING TAKEN ADVANTAGE OF BY IRVING, THE SEXIST PIG?

NO, ANDREA.

YOU MEAN YOU'VE FINALLY REALIZED YOU'RE AN INDIVIDUAL WITH RIGHTS AND NEEDS OF YOUR OWN ???

YOU MEAN YOU'VE FINALLY LIBERATED YOURSELF FROM DOMINANCE ?! YOU MEAN YOU'RE ACTUALLY BECOMING YOUR OWN PERSON ?!!!?!

NOT EXACTLY..... I MEAN HE HASN'T CALLED ME LATELY.

58

I'LL SHOW THAT STUPID RESTAURANT!

THEY MADE ME REALIZE HOW HARD IT IS FOR A LADY TO GO OUT TO DINNER BY HERSELF IN A CHAUVINISTIC WORLD!

I'M GOING TO **PROVE** THAT I'D GET BETTER SERVICE IF I WERE A MAN!!

SORRY, SIR. I CAN'T LET YOU IN WITHOUT A TIE.

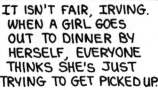

IT ISN'T FAIR, IRVING. WHEN A GIRL GOES OUT TO DINNER BY HERSELF, EVERYONE THINKS SHE'S JUST TRYING TO GET PICKED UP.

YEA? WELL, HOW DO YOU THINK A **GUY** FEELS WHEN HE GOES OUT TO DINNER BY HIMSELF?!!

THAT'S DIFFERENT, IRVING.

YOU **ARE** TRYING TO GET PICKED UP.

I **HATE** PAYING FOR MY OWN MOVIE TICKET, IRVING!

THAT'S THE NEW EQUALITY, CATHY.

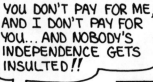

YOU DON'T PAY FOR ME, AND I DON'T PAY FOR YOU... AND NOBODY'S INDEPENDENCE GETS INSULTED!!

UH, OH. I FORGOT MY WALLET.

ONE, PLEASE.

PLEASE, MOM. NOT ANOTHER BLIND DATE WITH ONE OF YOUR FRIEND'S KIDS.

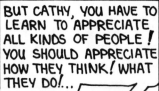

BUT CATHY, YOU HAVE TO LEARN TO APPRECIATE ALL KINDS OF PEOPLE! YOU SHOULD APPRECIATE HOW THEY THINK! WHAT THEY DO!...

I KNOW, MOM. I REMEMBER THE LAST ONE YOU FIXED ME UP WITH.

HE MADE ME APPRECIATE SPENDING SATURDAY NIGHTS IRONING SOCKS.

For those of us who have kept our mouths shut during the crucial moments of most of our lives, these are not easy times.

All of a sudden, we're supposed to be able to lay out our most private feelings with the naturalness of saying, "good morning." And if that weren't hard enough, we're suddenly supposed to be prepared to deal with the consequences of both speaking and hearing the truth.

Cathy struggles constantly to express her feelings and to get the people around her to express theirs. Or, more realistically, to get them to express the feelings she wants to hear. Having an active fantasy life, and a talent for rationalizing away every unpleasantry, she often finds escapes just too tempting.

After all, in the face of an open, honest confrontation of feelings that you know will result in breaking up, who wouldn't wonder just how important it is to bring all this up right now? Who wouldn't be tempted to sneak back to the sweet security of silence? Who wouldn't be moved to— just this once — just take the stupid phone off the hook?

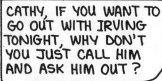

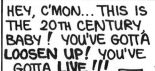

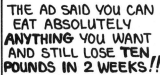

1. LOSE 10 POUNDS.
2. QUIT SMOKING.

3. GROW MY NAILS.
4. BECOME A WITTY CONVERSATIONALIST.

I HATE IT WHEN MY SUMMER GOALS ARE THE SAME AS MY WINTER GOALS.

I THINK THE WOMEN'S MOVEMENT IS REALLY HAVING AN EFFECT ON ME, ANDREA.

YEA?

YEA. I USED TO FEEL GUILTY ABOUT **NOT** CLEANING THE APARTMENT.

NOW I FEEL GUILTY WHEN I **DO**.

YOU'RE REALLY GOING TO BE SORRY IF YOU KEEP LAYING OUT IN THE SUN EVERY DAY, CATHY.

WHY, MOM?

IT'S GOING TO MAKE YOUR SKIN WRINKLE PREMATURELY.

YOU MEAN I SHOULD SPEND THE PRIME YEARS OF MY YOUTH WITH PASTY WHITE SKIN SO I'LL LOOK NICE WHEN I'M 86??

UH HUH.

WHO'S GOING TO CARE WHEN I'M 86?!!!?

HI CATHY. THIS IS EMERSON. DO YOU WANT TO GO OUT?

C'MON, EMERSON. NO ONE **EVER** ASKS ME OUT!

I'M **ASKING**. YOU WANT TO GO OUT?

WHAT ARE YOU TRYING TO DO? RUIN MY REPUTATION?

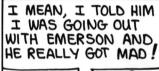

BUT WHY DID "FOOT BEAUTIFUL" MAGAZINE SEND **ME** ALL THESE SUBSCRIPTIONS, ANDREA? HOW'D THEY EVEN GET MY ADDRESS??

CATHY, YOUR NAME IS ON **THOUSANDS** OF LISTS!

COMPANIES ALL OVER THE COUNTRY KNOW YOUR ADDRESS!!.... **MILLIONS** OF PEOPLE HAVE ACCESS TO YOUR PHONE NUMBER EVERY DAY!!!

IT REALLY MAKES YOU WONDER, DOESN'T IT?!?

YEAH.

I WONDER WHY I DON'T GET MORE CALLS.

DO YOU HAVE ANY IDEA HOW BORING IT IS TO EAT NUTRITIOUS MEALS WHEN YOU'RE SINGLE, MOM??

IT'S BORING TO SHOP FOR THE FOOD... IT'S BORING TO COOK THE FOOD... IT'S BORING TO SERVE THE FOOD... AND IT'S BORING TO DO THE DISHES!!!

BUT CATHY, IF YOU JUST ATE WELL-BALANCED MEALS, YOU WOULDN'T EAT SO MUCH JUNK FOOD.

YES I WOULD.

I ALWAYS EAT JUNK WHEN I'M BORED.

IRVING, DO YOU THINK THE MAGIC HAS GONE OUT OF OUR RELATIONSHIP?

NOBODY EVER LOOKS AT ME, ANDREA.

WELL, GIVE YOURSELF SOME PIZAZZ, CATHY.

WEAR SOME KICKY NEW CLOTHES! PUT FLOWERS IN YOUR HAIR!

LET YOUR FEET DANCE WHEN YOU WALK! LET YOUR ATTITUDE SING!!

I COULDN'T DO THAT, ANDREA.

EVERYBODY WOULD LOOK AT ME.

85

IS THIS THE LINE FOR "THE GOODBYE GIRL"?

I GUESS SO. EVERYONE'S STANDING HERE.

DIDN'T YOU WONDER WHY NO ONE'S IN THAT LINE?? DIDN'T YOU GO UP AND ASK??

ANDREA, IF I WENT ALL THE WAY UP THERE AND IT TURNED OUT I WAS WRONG, I'D FEEL STUPID.

BUT WHAT IF ALL THESE PEOPLE ARE WRONG?! WOULDN'T YOU FEEL EVEN MORE STUPID FOR STAYING HERE??!

NO.

SOMEHOW IT'S BETTER TO BE PART OF A STUPID GROUP, THAN TO BE THE ONE STUPID INDIVIDUAL.

HOW ABOUT A DRINK?

OKAY. I'LL HAVE A PEPSI.

NO...I MEAN A **DRINK** DRINK. DON'T YOU WANT TO GET HAPPY?

DRINKING PEPSI MAKES ME HAPPY.

NO, I MEAN **HAPPY** HAPPY. C'MON, I'LL BUY.

YOU MEAN YOU'LL **BUY** BUY?

YEAH, BUY BUY.

BYE BYE.

PLEASE SEND MY HAMBURGER BACK, MISS. IT ISN'T DONE LIKE I ORDERED.

YOU WANT TO SEND YOUR HAMBURGER BACK? HA, HA, HA!!

SHE WANTS TO SEND HER HAMBURGER BACK! HA, HA, HA, HA!!

SOMETHING TELLS ME YOU'RE NOT SUPPOSED TO ASSERT YOURSELF UNLESS YOU'RE SPENDING MORE THAN 59¢ FOR LUNCH.

WHAT'S THIS??

THIS IS YOUR #7.

GEE, IN THE PICTURE ON THE MENU, IT LOOKED LIKE THE #7 WAS A BIG JUICY STEAK SURROUNDED BY FRIED ONIONS AND CUTE LITTLE TOMATOES.

OH YEAH??

WELL, IN THE PICTURE, THE PERSON **EATING** THE #7 IS A GORGEOUS BLOND SURROUNDED BY FOOTBALL PLAYERS.

ONE OF US IS AN IMPOSTER.

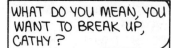

WHY WON'T YOU GO OUT WITH EMERSON NOW THAT YOU'RE NOT SEEING IRVING ANYMORE, CATHY?

I DON'T WANT TO GO OUT WITH A GUY THAT IRVING ALREADY KNOWS ABOUT, ANDREA.

CATHY, IRVING NEVER EVEN CONSIDERED EMERSON A THREAT **BEFORE** YOU BROKE UP! THAT DOESN'T MAKE SENSE!!

YES IT DOES.

WHAT'S THE POINT OF DATING SOMEONE WHO DOESN'T MAKE THE GUY YOU BROKE UP WITH JEALOUS?

YOU REALLY SHOULD COME TO MY WOMEN'S GROUP SINCE YOU'VE BROKEN UP WITH IRVING, CATHY.

FOR WHAT ANDREA?

WE CAN HELP YOU LEARN TO USE YOUR NEW FREE TIME FOR SELF-DISCOVERY AND GOAL SEEKING. YOU'LL REALLY START TO APPRECIATE SPENDING TIME ALONE!

YOU MEAN A BUNCH OF YOU SIT AROUND DISCUSSING HOW TO TURN MISERY AND REJECTION INTO A MEANINGFUL EXPERIENCE??

WELL, SORT OF...

SOMEHOW, I THINK I'M ALREADY STARTING TO APPRECIATE SPENDING TIME ALONE.

OH ANDREA, WHAT HAVE I DONE WITH MY LIFE?

WHAT YOU **HAVE** DONE DOESN'T MATTER, CATHY.

IT'S WHAT YOU'RE **GOING** TO DO THAT COUNTS!!

OH ANDREA, WHAT AM I GOING TO DO WITH MY LIFE?

I'VE DECIDED TO TALK TO A CAREER COUNSELOR ABOUT FINDING A NEW CAREER, ANDREA.

SURE, SURE.

EVERY TIME YOU BREAK UP WITH IRVING YOU DECIDE TO MAKE SOME RADICAL CHANGE, AND THEN YOU CHICKEN OUT.

BUT I'M SERIOUS THIS TIME!

I'M ABOUT TO CREATE A WHOLE NEW LIFE FOR MYSELF!

NO YOU'RE NOT. YOU'RE GOING TO CHICKEN OUT LIKE YOU ALWAYS DO.

NO ONE EVER TAKES A FORMER CHICKEN SERIOUSLY.

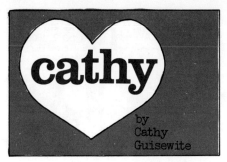

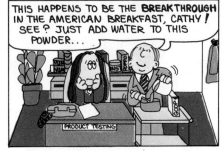

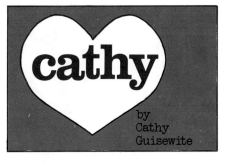

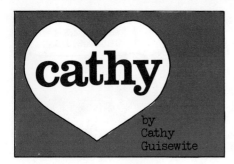

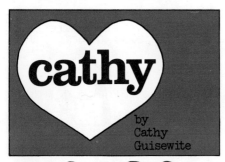

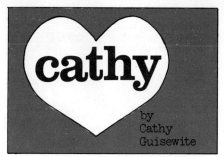

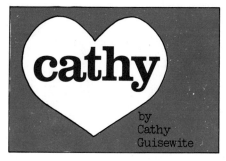

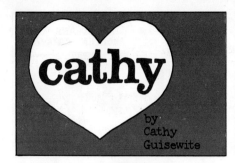

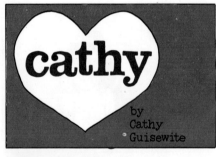

The new heroines of every newspaper are the ones with dynamic careers, not spotless floors. The most conventional women's magazines now feature "Fourteen Ways to Liberate Yourself from the Kitchen" right after "Fourteen Exciting Things to do with Leftover Hamburger." Even the ladies in the laundry soap commercials are getting their husbands to help.

The women's movement is everywhere, presenting important new options for every part of our lives. It's no wonder that some of us feel confused; that we should find ourselves, like Cathy, floundering in the middle of two ideals.

While the extremes between the independent, assertive career woman and the sweet little housewife seem miles apart, the choices aren't so clear-cut for any of us. At some point, each of us has to decide which of the old values we're really willing to part with. And which of the new philosophies we believe in strongly enough to actually live.

With her mother rooting for the old, and her girlfriend, Andrea, rooting for the new, Cathy is faced with the dilemma that many of us feel: *Now* what am I supposed to do?

I hope that watching Cathy struggle to make some changes in her life will encourage you to not give up if you fall a bit short of becoming instantly liberated. That she'll help you see the humor in being someone's decidedly unliberated mother. And most of all, that she'll help you consider a most serious subject and feel like laughing instead of ripping your hair out.

CONGRATULATIONS, CATHY. I JUST SIGNED YOU UP FOR MY ASSERTIVENESS TRAINING WORKSHOP!

OH NO, ANDREA. NOT ANOTHER ONE OF YOUR SELF-IMPROVEMENT COURSES.

CATHY, THIS HAPPENS TO BE THE ONE COURSE THAT'S REALLY HELPING WOMEN BREAK THRU THE CHAINS OF A MALE-ORIENTED WORLD!!

THIS IS THE COURSE THAT WILL RAISE YOUR SELF-ESTEEM! THIS IS THE COURSE THAT WILL TEACH YOU TO SAY NO WITHOUT FEAR OF REJECTION!!!

NO.

WELCOME TO ASSERTIVENESS TRAINING. EVERY ONE OF YOU HAS MADE THE FIRST BIG STEP TOWARDS ASSERTIVENESS BY COMING HERE.

ASSERTIVENESS TRAINING WORKSHOP

YOU'VE DECIDED YOU ARE NOT BODIES WITHOUT MINDS!! YOU ARE NOT SLAVES WITHOUT PAYCHECKS!!

BY COMING HERE TONIGHT, YOU'RE SAYING YOU'RE ALL SOMETHING MUCH MORE VITAL TO OUR SOCIETY!!

YEA... GIRLS WITHOUT DATES.

IN ASSERTIVENESS TRAINING EXERCISE #1, EACH OF YOU WILL WRITE YOUR GOOD QUALITIES ON 3x5 CARDS...PIN THEM TO YOUR SHIRT...AND WALK AROUND THE ROOM LOOKING AT EACH OTHER.

I CAN'T DO THAT, ANDREA!

YOU HAVE TO, CATHY! YOU CAN'T BEGIN TO BE ASSERTIVE UNTIL YOU REALIZE YOU HAVE GOOD THINGS TO OFFER!!

ASSERTIVENESS TRAINING WORKSHOP

I'LL FEEL STUPID!!!

DO IT, CATHY!!!

LOVELY BRIGHT SWEET

COOPERATIVE

CUTE SMART SEXY WITTY

LITTLE BOYS ARE ALWAYS ENCOURAGED TO BOAST ABOUT THEIR ACHIEVEMENTS ...WHILE LITTLE GIRLS ARE SCOLDED FOR BOASTING BECAUSE IT'S "UNFEMININE"

ASSERTIVENESS TRAINING WORKSHOP

BUT WITH ASSERTIVENESS TRAINING EXERCISE #2, WOMEN CAN REDISCOVER THE PRIDE THAT WE HAVE EVERY RIGHT TO EXPRESS!

ASSERTIVENESS TRAINING WORKSHOP

EACH ONE OF YOU WILL NOW STAND UP AND SAY OUT LOUD THE ONE THING YOU'RE MOST PROUD OF ABOUT YOURSELF!

ASSERTIVENESS TRAINING WORKSHOP

I AM VERY PROUD OF THE FACT THAT I HAVE NEVER BOASTED.

ASSERTIVENESS TRAINING WORKSHOP

MANY WOMEN HAVE A PROBLEM CRITICIZING LOVED ONES FOR FEAR THEY'LL BE REJECTED.

ASSERTIVENESS TRAINING WORKSHOP

BUT IN ASSERTIVENESS TRAINING, WE LEARN THAT CRITICISM IS GOOD FOR RELATIONSHIPS!! THAT CRITICISM DOES NOT MEAN REJECTION!!

FOR EXAMPLE, CATHY, TELL US THE ONE THING YOU'D MOST LIKE TO CRITICIZE YOUR BOYFRIEND IRVING FOR.

REJECTING ME.

ASSERTIVENESS TRAINING WORKSHOP

WHAT DO YOU MEAN YOU DON'T LIKE MY ASSERTIVENESS TRAINING WORKSHOP, CATHY??!!

I JUST DON'T KNOW IF I WANT TO LEARN HOW TO BE THAT STRONG, ANDREA.

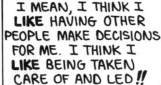

I MEAN, I THINK I LIKE HAVING OTHER PEOPLE MAKE DECISIONS FOR ME. I THINK I LIKE BEING TAKEN CARE OF AND LED!!

WHAT?!

ANDREA, DEEP DOWN, I THINK I REALLY LIKE TO BE PUSHED AROUND!!

AAAUGHH!!!

I THINK I JUST ASSERTED MYSELF.

I DON'T GET IT, ANDREA. THE WHOLE POINT OF ASSERTIVENESS TRAINING IS LEARNING TO EXPRESS HOW YOU REALLY FEEL, RIGHT?

RIGHT!!

SO WHY IS IT SO HORRIBLE IF I SAY I REALLY FEEL THAT I DON'T WANT TO ASSERT MYSELF???

ASSERTIVENESS TRAINING WORKSHOP

DON'T DO THIS TO ME, CATHY.

ASSERTIVENESS TRAINING WORKSHOP

THE BEST WAY TO LEARN TO ASSERT YOURSELF WITH IRVING IS TO PRACTICE WHEN HE ISN'T HERE, CATHY.

NOW PRETEND THAT THIS CHAIR IS IRVING...HE SAID HE'D PICK YOU UP AT 8:00, BUT HE JUST SHOWED UP AN HOUR AND A HALF LATE.

WHAT ARE YOU GOING TO SAY THAT REALLY EXPRESSES HOW YOU FEEL WHEN YOU FIRST SEE HIM??!!

YOU FORGOT TO DUST YOURSELF, IRVING.

BUT I HATE PARTIES, ANDREA! ALL THE PEOPLE INTIMIDATE ME!

THEY WON'T TONIGHT, CATHY.

TONIGHT **YOU'RE** GOING TO **STAND OUT** AS A VIVACIOUS STUDENT OF ASSERTIVENESS TRAINING!!!

HEADS WILL TURN TO WATCH **YOU**! CONVERSATIONS WILL STOP TO LISTEN TO WHAT **YOU** HAVE TO SAY!!

FORGET IT, ANDREA.

NOW **I'M** INTIMIDATING ME.

WHAT DO YOU MEAN YOU'RE NOT COMING TO DINNER TONIGHT, IRVING?! **YOU'RE A ROTTEN, DUMB CREEP**!!!

THERE, ANDREA! HOW WAS **THAT** FOR ASSERTING MYSELF?!!

THAT WASN'T ASSERTIVE BEHAVIOR, CATHY. THAT WAS **AGGRESSIVE** BEHAVIOR.

ASSERTING YOURSELF MEANS EXPLAINING **WHY** YOU'RE MAD ABOUT SOMETHING... NOT CLOBBERING THE GUY WITH INSULTS!!

I KNEW IT FELT TOO GOOD TO HAVE THE SUPPORT OF AN ORGANIZATION.

HOW'S YOUR HAMBURGER, ANDREA? MINE'S NOT THAT GREAT.

AHAH! THEN SEND IT BACK!!

NO... IT'S NOT **THAT** BAD.

CATHY, I DRAGGED YOU TO 10 ASSERTIVENESS TRAINING CLASSES SO YOU WOULDN'T LET YOURSELF BE TAKEN ADVANTAGE OF LIKE THIS!

NOW SEND THAT HAMBURGER BACK! DEMAND TO GET WHAT YOU'RE PAYING FOR!! **ASSERT YOURSELF, CATHY**!!!

I CAN'T ASSERT MYSELF ON AN EMPTY STOMACH.

I HAD MY BIG CHANCE TO USE ASSERTIVENESS TRAINING TODAY, ANDREA ...THE GARAGE SAID MY CAR WOULD BE READY TODAY, BUT WHEN I GOT THERE, THEY SAID THEY'D FOUND 14 MORE THINGS WRONG WITH IT.

DID YOU LET THEM HAVE IT?!

YOU BET I DID! I TOLD THEM I WAS SICK AND TIRED OF GETTING RIPPED OFF BY CAR SERVICE PLACES JUST BECAUSE I'M A WOMAN!!

I DEMANDED TO SEE THE OWNER SO I COULD TELL HIM HOW HIS SEXIST OPERATION HAD JUST CAUSED HIM TO LOSE A CUSTOMER!!

AND???

ANDREA, THE OWNER WAS A WOMAN!!

NO WONDER WE'RE RIDING THE BUS.

CITY BUS

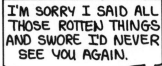

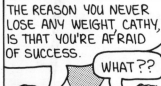

OKAY, ANDREA. HERE WE ARE AT MIRAC-O-SPA.

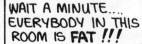
WAIT A MINUTE.... EVERYBODY IN THIS ROOM IS FAT!!!

WHAT DID YOU EXPECT??

I EXPECTED ROOMS FULL OF TRIM BODIES! FLAT STOMACHS! FIRM THIGHS!

CATHY, THESE PEOPLE ARE JUST LIKE YOU. THEY PROBABLY JUST STARTED TONIGHT, TOO.

HI. I'M PHOEBE, YOUR INSTRUCTOR.

HI. HOW MUCH DO YOU WEIGH?

WHAT DO YOU CARE, PHOEBE?

WELL, HERE AT MIRAC-O-SPA, WE CALL YOU BY YOUR WEIGHT INSTEAD OF BY YOUR FIRST NAME.

WHAT?!

IT'S AN EXTRA INCENTIVE TO GET THOSE POUNDS OFF FAST, BECAUSE IT FORCES YOU TO ACKNOWLEDGE JUST HOW OVERWEIGHT YOU REALLY ARE!!

OH YEA? WHAT DO THEY CALL YOU?

PHOEBE.

REGULATION DRESS AT MIRAC-O-SPA IS THIS PURPLE LEOTARD.

YOU'VE GOT TO BE KIDDING! I'LL LOOK LIKE AN EGGPLANT IN THIS THING!!

NOW, NOW, CATHY. UNTIL YOU REACH YOUR GOAL, HOW YOU LOOK ON THE OUTSIDE DOESN'T MATTER ...IT'S HOW YOU FEEL ON THE INSIDE THAT COUNTS.

I'LL FEEL LIKE AN EGGPLANT.

I CAN'T BELIEVE YOU'RE ACTUALLY GOING THRU WITH A MEMBERSHIP AT MIRAC-O-SPA, CATHY. YOU CAN'T AFFORD IT.

WELL, THE LADY POINTED OUT TO ME THAT IF I SPEND THAT MUCH ON A MEMBERSHIP, THE GUILT WILL REALLY DRIVE ME TO USE THE PLACE.

SHE SAID THAT WHEN I SEE HOW FAST MY INCHES DISAPPEAR, IT'LL BE WORTH ANY PRICE..... ...ANDREA, IT'S GOT TO MAKE ME LOSE WEIGHT!

I JUST SPENT MY WHOLE YEAR'S FOOD BUDGET ON IT.

I CAN'T BELIEVE IT, PHOEBE. I'VE BEEN COMING TO MIRAC·O·SPA FOR A SOLID WEEK AND I HAVEN'T LOST A SINGLE INCH.

YOU CAN'T EXPECT TO **SEE** PROGRESS INSTANTLY, CATHY. IT HAPPENS **INSIDE** FIRST!

YOU'RE WORKING THOSE MUSCLES! **BUILDING STAMINA AND STRENGTH!!**

JUST WHAT I ALWAYS WANTED.

STRONG FAT.

WHY AREN'T YOU AT MIRAC·O·SPA TONIGHT, CATHY?

I QUIT.

YOU **CAN'T** QUIT! YOU SIGNED UP FOR A **YEAR**!

ANDREA, I HAVE BEEN SHRIVELED UP BY THEIR SAUNA... I'VE BEEN STRETCHED UNTIL I COULD SCREAM BY THEIR EXERCISE MACHINES...

AND I'M STARVING TO DEATH ON THE DIET THEY PUT ME ON !!!

YEA? WELL, HOW DO YOU THINK YOU'RE GOING TO GET OUT OF IT ??

FOR STARTERS, I'M GOING TO EAT MY CONTRACT.

WHY AREN'T YOU GOING OUT WITH IRVING TONIGHT, CATHY?

YOU JUST DON'T UNDERSTAND OUR RELATIONSHIP, MOM.

IRVING DOESN'T HAVE TO TAKE ME OUT EVERY SINGLE NIGHT. I DON'T CARE IF HE DOESN'T VISIT ME OR CALL TEN TIMES A DAY.

I JUST **NEED** HIM. I JUST NEED TO KNOW HE'S **THERE**!

WHERE?!!

DON'T GET TECHNICAL.

HERBAL ESSENCE SHAMPOO...

ROSE WATER CREME RINSE...

MUSK OIL SHOWER COLOGNE...

HOW COME I SMELL LIKE SOMEBODY'S ATTIC?

106

CATHY, I....
FORGET IT, IRVING! IT DOESN'T COUNT IF YOU SAY YOU LOVE ME AFTER I'VE PLEADED WITH YOU TO DO IT!!!

OKAY, OKAY. SAY IT! IT COUNTS!!

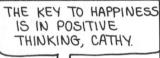
THE KEY TO HAPPINESS IS IN POSITIVE THINKING, CATHY.

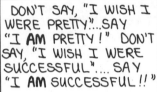
DON'T SAY, "I WISH I WERE PRETTY"...SAY "I AM PRETTY!" DON'T SAY, "I WISH I WERE SUCCESSFUL".... SAY "I AM SUCCESSFUL!!"

YOU MEAN WHEN I'M ON A DIET I SHOULDN'T SAY "I WISH I WERE THIN ENOUGH TO EAT THIS DONUT"?
THAT'S RIGHT. IF YOU THINK POSITIVELY YOU'LL SAY...

I AM THIN ENOUGH TO EAT THIS DONUT!

CATHY, YOUR CUPBOARDS ARE PRACTICALLY EMPTY.
THAT'S RIGHT, ANDREA.

I HAVE RID MY KITCHEN OF ALL COOKIES, CANDY, DONUTS AND PRETZELS. FROM NOW ON, THIS IS GOING TO BE A HEALTHY KITCHEN!!

WOW CATHY! I'M REALLY PROUD!! YOU'VE FINALLY PUT JUNK FOOD IN ITS PLACE!!!
THAT'S RIGHT, ANDREA.

I HID IT ALL UNDER MY BED.

BARS ARE SO SUPERFICIAL AND TACKY.

BARS ARE SO PLASTIC AND SHALLOW.

BARS ARE SO PHONEY.

BARS ARE THE ONLY PLACE IN THE WORLD WHERE EVERYONE TRIES TO IMPRESS EACH OTHER BY SAYING WHAT A DUMB WAY THEY'VE JUST CHOSEN TO SPEND THEIR TIME.

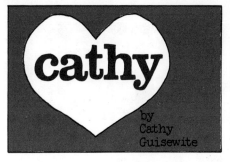

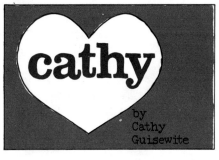

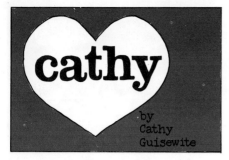

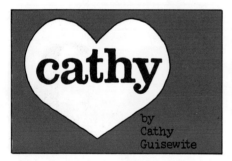

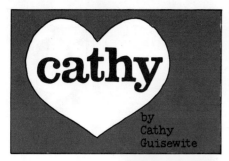

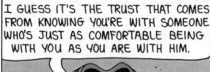

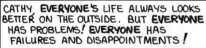

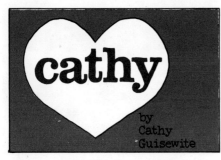

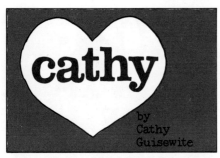

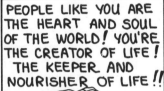

C'MON, MOM. YOU'VE GOT TO GET OUT OF THIS DEPRESSION.

YOU JUST DON'T REALIZE WHAT A SPECIAL PERSON IT TAKES TO BE A GOOD HOUSEWIFE AND MOTHER!

WHAT'S SO SPECIAL ABOUT IT, CATHY?

WELL, YOU TELL ME. JUST TELL ME ALL THE THINGS YOU ACCOMPLISHED TODAY!

I WENT TO THE SUPERMARKET AND FOUND A CART THAT DIDN'T HAVE A BROKEN WHEEL.

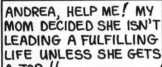

ANDREA, HELP ME! MY MOM DECIDED SHE ISN'T LEADING A FULFILLING LIFE UNLESS SHE GETS A JOB!!

RIGHT ON, CATHY!

ANDREA, THIS IS MY MOTHER WE'RE TALKING ABOUT HERE! NOT SOME HIP CHICK!!

RIGHT ON!

BUT IF MY MOM GETS A JOB, WHAT'S LEFT OF TRADITION?! WHO CAN I LOOK TO FOR THE SACRED VALUES OF HOME AND FAMILY?!!!

RIGHT ON! RIGHT ON!

HELLO, DADDY?

OKAY, MOM. IF YOU'RE DETERMINED TO GET A JOB, LET'S FIGURE OUT WHAT YOU'RE QUALIFIED FOR.

NOTHING.

SURE YOU ARE. IN ONE DAY YOU CAN DO FIVE LOADS OF LAUNDRY, VACUUM AND DUST AN ENTIRE HOUSE, DO TWO WEEKS OF SHOPPING, PAY BILLS, AND...

WHAT'S WRONG, CATHY?

I THINK MAYBE YOU'RE RIGHT.

CAN I INTEREST YOU IN A MAKE-UP MIRROR?

THIS DELUXE MODEL HAS SEPARATE SETTINGS FOR MORNING LIGHT, AFTERNOON LIGHT, AND EVENING LIGHT.

DOES THIS MEAN I CAN TELL WHAT TIME IT IS BY LOOKING AT MY FACE?

114

I HAVE SMEARED MY FACE WITH AVOCADO RINDS FOR SOFTNESS...

I HAVE DUMPED LEMON AND EGG ON MY HAIR FOR SHINE...

MY ELBOWS ARE CAKED IN COCOA-BUTTER FOR SMOOTHNESS...

HOW COME I NEVER LOOK GOOD ENOUGH TO EAT?

WHAT AM I GOING TO DO, ANDREA??!!!

EVERYBODY'S DASHING OFF TO THE SWIMMING POOL -- AND I'M SO FAT, I'M HUMILIATED TO BE SEEN IN MY BATHING SUIT!!!

WELL, WHAT ARE YOU GOING TO DO ABOUT IT, CATHY?!!!

PRAY FOR RAIN.

MMM...THICK MASHED POTATOES...HOT BUTTERY ROLLS...GOOEY MACARONI SALAD...

STEAMING APPLE PIE... ...ICE CREAM SMOTHERED IN HOT FUDGE SAUCE AND PEANUTS...

HI, CATHY.

WE KNOW HOW HARD YOU'RE TRYING TO DIET, SO I FIXED US A NICE ASPARAGUS CASSEROLE FOR DINNER.

THERE'S NOTHING WORSE THAN BEING HANDED SOMETHING DIETETIC WHEN YOU'RE MENTALLY PREPARED TO PIG OUT.

I MET ANOTHER GUY ON THE ELEVATOR TODAY, ANDREA.

OH NO, CATHY. NOT ANOTHER INSURANCE SALESMAN.

THIS YOUNG MAN HAPPENS TO BE VERY BRIGHT. HE SAID HE READS DOONESBURY EVERY DAY.

BIG DEAL. MILLIONS OF PEOPLE READ DOONESBURY EVERY DAY!!

YEA. BUT HE UNDERSTANDS IT EVERY DAY.

Everyone knows that beauty has more to do with the inside of a person than the outside. Still, if someone even suggests that a new kind of lipstick will make me irresistible, I will rush out in the middle of the night to buy it, without batting an eye. I was only too happy to pass this compulsion along to Cathy, because it's one of the biggest threats to contentment that everyone has to deal with.

It's just too easy to believe that everyone in the world is perfect except you. To fall into the trap of measuring your self-worth through someone else's eyes. And to clutch onto the hope that something you buy will make it all better.

121

Cathy is more than eager to wrap up her hopes for happiness in everything from dish soap to mascara. She turns any suggestion of a benefit into the complete solution for every teeny problem. And when the product doesn't deliver the miracle she burdens it with, she's quick to be cynical and to blame the creme rinse for letting her down.

We all frantically try to be like everyone else, yet dream of being special. We want to believe we're beautiful just as we are, but we snatch up the latest fashions and fragrances, just in case. We wink and flirt with the mirror at home, and then get to the party and are embarrassed by what we're wearing.

Even Cathy knows you can't buy happiness with a new tube of lipstick. . . but for only $1.29, why not give it a shot?

OOH, BOY, ANDREA! I'VE GOT TO GET SOME OF THAT "CREAMY-DREAMY LIPSTICK"!!!

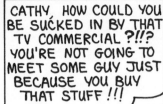

CATHY, HOW COULD YOU BE SUCKED IN BY THAT TV COMMERCIAL?!!? YOU'RE NOT GOING TO MEET SOME GUY JUST BECAUSE YOU BUY THAT STUFF!!!

THAT'S CHAUVINISTIC CAPITALISM AT IT'S WORST!! ALL THEY'RE SELLING IS SEX, HOPE AND DREAMS!!

I'LL TAKE IT!

I AM BEAUTIFUL.

THAT'S GOOD, CATHY. POSITIVE REINFORCEMENT WILL REALLY MAKE YOU FEEL BETTER ABOUT YOURSELF.

I'M BEAUTIFUL, BEAUTIFUL, BEAUTIFUL.

GOOD, CATHY! SAY IT TILL YOU MEAN IT.

I AM BEAUTIFUL! I AM BEAUTIFUL!! I AM BEAUTIFUL!!

YOU'RE BEAUTIFUL!

WHAT'S THE MATTER?

I JUST REMEMBERED WHAT I LOOK LIKE.

SHAMPOO...HOT OIL TREATMENT...PROTEIN CONDITIONER...CREME RINSE...

...TANGLE RELAXANT... ...SETTING LOTION... ...HAIR SPRAY...

NO WONDER EVERYBODY'S STARTED WASHING THEIR HAIR EVERY DAY.

BY THE TIME YOU'RE DONE PUTTING ALL THIS STUFF ON IT, IT'S FILTHY AGAIN.

OH CATHY, WE HAVE SO MUCH TO DO AS WOMEN!

I KNOW, ANDREA.

SO MANY NEW DOORS TO OPEN! SO MANY NEW THINGS TO DISCOVER!!

I KNOW, I KNOW.

WHAT NEW AVENUE SHOULD WE EXPLORE TODAY???

WELL, I DON'T KNOW ABOUT YOU..

.....I WAS GOING TO LOOK FOR A KIND OF MASCARA THAT DOESN'T MAKE MY EYELASHES STICK TOGETHER.

CATHY, IF IRVING CAN KEEP FIVE RELATIONSHIPS WITH DIFFERENT GIRLS GOING ALL AT THE SAME TIME, WHY CAN'T YOU FEEL COMFORTABLE DOING THE SAME THING??

DON'T YOU THINK YOU HAVE THE SAME KIND OF RIGHTS??

OF COURSE I HAVE THE SAME KIND OF RIGHTS, ANDREA.

I JUST DON'T HAVE THE SAME KIND OF MEMORY.

THANKS, CATHY. I WAS DESPERATE FOR SOME CLEAN CLOTHES.

WELL?

WELL WHAT?

AREN'T YOU GOING TO SAY ANYTHING ABOUT THE APRIL-FRESH SCENT??

AREN'T YOU GOING TO MENTION THE SOFT, NON-STATIC FEEL?? AREN'T YOU GOING TO MARVEL THAT YOUR WHITES LOOK WHITER, YOUR BRIGHTS LOOK BRIGHTER?

AREN'T YOU GOING TO NOTICE THAT EVEN YOUR PERMANENT PRESS LOOKS LIKE NEW AGAIN??!!

YOU'RE EATING FRENCH FRIES WITH YOUR HAMBURGER, CATHY! I THOUGHT YOU WERE ON A DIET!

IT'S OKAY, ANDREA. I'M NOT GOING TO EAT THE BUN.

A MILKSHAKE, TOO?!

ANDREA, I TOLD YOU. I'M NOT TOUCHING THE BUN.

CATHY, THIS DOESN'T MAKE SENSE! YOU'RE GOING TO WIND UP EATING 5 TIMES AS MUCH!!

NEVER EXPECT A SKINNY PERSON TO UNDERSTAND THE SIGNIFICANCE OF NOT EATING THE BUN.

YOU KNOW WHY YOUR DIETS ALWAYS FAIL, CATHY? YOU FORGET ALL ABOUT TRYING TO LEARN TO EAT RIGHT. YOU FORGET THAT YOU'RE SUPPOSED TO BE RE-EDUCATING YOUR EATING HABITS!

YOU FORGET WHAT YOUR GOAL REALLY IS!!

I KNOW WHAT MY GOAL IS, ANDREA.

I WANT TO GET SO SKINNY THAT PEOPLE WILL BEG ME TO EAT.

AND THEN WHAT?

THEN I'LL EAT!!

LOVE IS NOT MAKING HIM MOVE, EVEN WHEN YOUR ARM FALLS ASLEEP.

HI. I'D LIKE TO BUY SOME COLOGNE FOR MY BOYFRIEND.

FINE, WHAT WOULD YOU LIKE? "MACHO" "STUD", "SEX", "VIRILE", OR "HE-MAN"?

DON'T YOU HAVE ANY "THOUGHFUL", "ROMANTIC" OR "SWEET"?

WE COULDN'T SELL COLOGNES WITH NAMES LIKE THAT, LADY!

A GUY WOULD BE EMBARRASSED TO SAY WHAT HE WAS WEARING!!

HEY, CATHY, WILL YOU GET ME A BEER?

HAH! DOESN'T HE KNOW THAT WOMEN DON'T HAVE TO ACT LIKE SLAVES ANYMORE?!

DOESN'T HE REALIZE THE NEW WOMAN DOES NOT MEASURE HER WORTH BY HOW SHE PLEASES HER MAN??!

DOESN'T HE KNOW OUR ENTIRE SOCIAL STRUCTURE IS MOVING TOWARD A WHOLE NEW KIND OF EQUALITY AND RESPECT?!!!

WELL??

I FORGOT THE QUESTION.

IRVING, DO YOU THINK WE HAVE A TOGETHER RELATIONSHIP OF THE 70'S?

SURE WE DO, CATHY.

WE'VE GOT NO STRINGS, NO TIES. YOU DO WHAT YOU WANT, I DO WHAT I WANT.

WE'RE **FREE**, CATHY! WE'RE **INDEPENDENT**!! WE'RE **ON OUR OWN**!!!

SOMEHOW I FELT MORE TOGETHER WHEN WE DIDN'T HAVE IT SO TOGETHER.

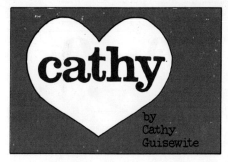

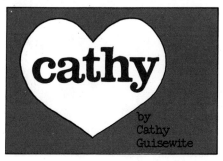

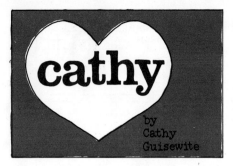

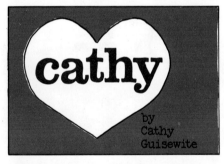

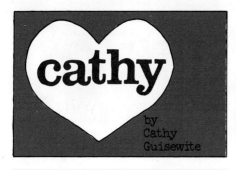

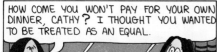

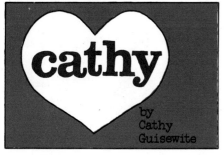

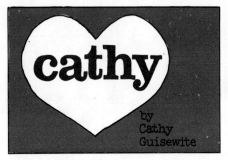

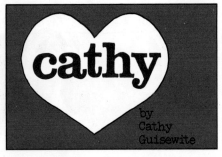

TRUST IS KNOWING THAT THE COMPANY YOU'RE HAVING WON'T PEEK BEHIND THE SHOWER CURTAIN TO SEE IF YOU'VE CLEANED THE BATHTUB RECENTLY.

WHY AREN'T YOU TALK-ING TO ME, IRVING? IS IT SOMETHING I SAID? IS IT SOME-THING I DID??

IS IT OVER BETWEEN US, IRVING?? WHAT HAPPENED?? WHAT WENT WRONG?? WHY ARE YOU BEING LIKE THIS??!!

I GOT MY HAIR CUT TODAY AND THE BARBER MADE IT TOO SHORT.

IT'S JUST LIKE A MAN TO BLAME EVERYTHING ON HIS HAIR.

I DON'T GET IT, IRVING. IF MY HAIR DOESN'T TURN OUT RIGHT ONE DAY AND I WANT TO SPEND 5 EXTRA MINUTES FIXING IT BEFORE WE GO OUT, YOU GO BERSERK.

BUT YOU SEE NOTHING WRONG WITH MOPING AROUND ABOUT YOUR STUPID HAIRCUT FOR AN ENTIRE WEEK!!

WHAT'S THE BIG DIFFERENCE??! IT'S MY HAIR!!!

GUYS ALWAYS HAVE A GREAT EXCUSE FOR MOPING LONGER THAN WOMEN.

YOUR HAIRCUT IS CUTE, IRVING CUTE?? THE BARBER SCALPED ME!!

I THINK IT'S CUTE. CATHY, EVEN IF HE'D GIVEN ME THE GREATEST HAIRCUT IN THE WORLD, CUTE ISN'T THE WORD YOU SHOULD USE TO DESCRIBE IT!

NO GUY WANTS TO BE TOLD HE HAS CUTE HAIR!! WE HATE CUTE!!!

IT LOOKS EVEN CUTER WHEN YOUR FACE TURNS PURPLE LIKE THAT. AAAUGH!!

STEP 1 TO MEETING THE CUTE GUY ACROSS THE ROOM: GIVE HIM A DEEP, SINCERE LOOK.

STEP 2: SMILE MEANINGFULLY, LETTING WARMTH AND MYSTERY EXUDE FROM YOUR BEING.

STEP 3: CHECK TO SEE THAT YOU HAVE NOT DONE STEP 2 WITH A HUNK OF CHEESEBURGER STUCK BETWEEN YOUR TEETH.

DON'T YOU SEE, CATHY? IF YOU PUT ALL YOUR ENERGY INTO A RELATIONSHIP WITH A MAN, AND THE MAN LEAVES, YOU'RE LEFT WITH NOTHING.

BUT IF YOU PUT THE SAME ENERGY INTO YOURSELF, YOU CAN'T LOSE! YOU'LL ALWAYS HAVE YOURSELF!!

THERE'S STILL ONE LITTLE PROBLEM, ANDREA.

MY SELF WANTS TO BE IN A RELATIONSHIP WITH A MAN.

LOOK AT ALL THESE NEW SUMMER CLASSES, CATHY. THERE ARE SELF-AWARENESS GROUPS TO HELP YOU DISCOVER WHO YOU REALLY ARE...

ENCOUNTER GROUPS, TO HELP YOU DEAL WITH WHO YOU REALLY ARE...

ASSERTIVENESS TRAINING GROUPS TO HELP YOU STAND UP FOR WHO YOU REALLY ARE...

SUDDENLY, THE ONLY WAY TO BECOME AN INDIVIDUAL IS TO JOIN A GROUP.

WHEN YOU'RE OLDER, YOU'LL LAUGH ABOUT ALL THIS, CATHY.

I KNOW, MOM.

WHEN YOU'RE OLDER, YOU'LL LAUGH ABOUT EVERYTHING YOU THINK IS SUCH A BIG PROBLEM.

I KNOW.

BUT IT JUST DOESN'T SEEM FAIR THAT I SHOULD HAVE TO WAIT FOR 10 YEARS TO SEE WHAT'S SO FUNNY.

NOW IS WHEN I NEED THE CHEERING UP.

JUST THINK, CATHY. WITH EQUALITY WOMEN WILL BE ABLE TO PURSUE THE SAME CAREERS AS MEN, WITHOUT DISCRIMINATION!

WE'LL BE PROTECTED BY THE SAME LEGAL RIGHTS AS MEN, WITHOUT QUESTION!!

WE'LL BE ABLE TO EARN AS MUCH AS MEN, WITHOUT FAIL!!

I THINK EQUALITY SHOULD GO EVEN FARTHER, ANDREA.

I WANT TO BE ABLE TO EAT AS MUCH AS MEN WITHOUT GETTING FAT.

WHY DON'T YOU GET SOME DECENT GLASSES AND SOME SILVERWARE THAT MATCHES, CATHY?

I'M WAITING TILL I GET MARRIED, ANDREA.

CATHY, THAT'S WRONG. A WOMAN SHOULDN'T POSTPONE GETTING NICE THINGS UNTIL SHE MEETS MR. WONDERFUL!

YOU SHOULDN'T WAIT FOR YOUR WEDDING DAY TO BETTER YOUR LIFE!!

I'M NOT WAITING FOR MY WEDDING DAY, ANDREA.

I'M WAITING FOR MY WEDDING PRESENTS.

IRVING, DO YOU FEEL CLOSER TO ME NOW THAN YOU DID ON OUR FIRST DATE?

SURE I DO, CATHY.

DO YOU FEEL CLOSER TO ME THAN YOU DID WHEN WE'D KNOWN EACH OTHER FOR A MONTH?

OF COURSE.

DO YOU THINK WE'RE CLOSER NOW THAN WE'VE EVER BEEN BEFORE?

NO QUESTION ABOUT IT.

THE CLOSER WE GET, THE FARTHER APART WE SIT.

I'M GETTING OLD, MOM.

DON'T BE SILLY, CATHY. YOU'RE A YOUNG WOMAN.

WELL, I THOUGHT SO. BUT WHEN I SEE MYSELF IN THE MIRROR, I DON'T LOOK LIKE I USED TO.

THAT'S ONLY NATURAL, CATHY.

BUT ONE LITTLE CHANGE OR TWO DOESN'T MEAN YOU'RE GETTING OLD.

I THINK IT'S MORE SERIOUS THAN THAT, MOM.

THIS MORNING I DIDN'T RECOGNIZE MY LEGS.

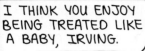

Panel 1: I THINK YOU ENJOY BEING TREATED LIKE A BABY, IRVING.

SO WHAT IF I DO, CATHY? A MAN **LIKES** TO HAVE LITTLE THINGS DONE FOR HIM.

Panel 2: HE LIKES TO BE PAMPERED AND FED AND TAKEN CARE OF.

Panel 3: THEN WHY WON'T YOU EVER LET ME DRIVE THE CAR WHEN WE GO OUT??

ARE YOU KIDDING?!

Panel 4: I'D FEEL LIKE I WAS RIDING AROUND WITH MY MOTHER!

Panel 5: SOMETIMES I JUST DON'T THINK IT'S GOING TO WORK OUT WITH IRVING, MOM.

WELL, IT'S OKAY IF IT DOESN'T.

Panel 6: THERE ARE MILLIONS OF OTHER MEN IN THE WORLD, CATHY.

Panel 7: YOU SHOULD ALWAYS REMEMBER THAT THERE IS NO ONE MAN WHO IS JUST RIGHT FOR YOU.

Panel 8: YOU'RE TELLING ME.

Panel 9: WHAT DO WE HAVE TO BE SO INDEPENDENT FOR, ANDREA?

WE JUST DO, CATHY.

Panel 10: WHEN A WOMAN IS FINANCIALLY AND EMOTIONALLY INDEPENDENT, HER LIFE WILL NEVER FALL APART IF ALL OF THE SUDDEN THERE ISN'T A MAN IN IT ANYMORE.

Panel 11: WHAT'S THE DIFFERENCE?

WOMEN'S STUDIES

Panel 12: MY LIFE FALLS APART WHEN THERE **IS** A MAN IN IT.

Panel 13: I SEE YOU'RE SCOTCH-TAPING YOUR BATHING SUIT TO THE REFRIGERATOR AGAIN, CATHY.

YES, ANDREA.

Panel 14: IT'S THE SUMMER DIET INCENTIVE RITUAL I LEARNED FROM MY FRIEND, CHRIS.

BUT, CATHY, IT NEVER WORKS!!

Panel 15: SURE IT DOES, ANDREA.

Panel 16: AS LONG AS MY BATHING SUIT IS STUCK TO THE REFRIGERATOR, I HAVE AN EXCUSE FOR NOT PUTTING IT ON.

YOU HAVE TO QUIT DREAMING, CATHY.

YOU HAVE TO QUIT PRETENDING THAT IRVING IS MR. WONDERFUL!

YOU HAVE TO QUIT MAKING YOUR RELATIONSHIP MORE IN YOUR FANTASY THAN IT CAN EVER BE IN REAL LIFE!!!

WHAT FOR?

IF IT'S NOT GOING TO HAPPEN ANYWAY, WHY NOT ENJOY IT WHERE I CAN?

SEE? I BELIEVE IN EQUALITY, CATHY. I'M COOKING THE STEAKS.

BIG DEAL, IRVING.

STEAK HAPPENS TO BE THE ONE THING IT'S ACCEPTABLE FOR A MAN TO COOK.

IF YOU WANT TO SHOW ME FREE THINKING, YOU MAKE THE JELLO SALAD MOLD.

BUT SWEETIE, I DON'T KNOW HOW.

HOW MANY PEOPLE DO YOU SUPPOSE THERE ARE IN THE WORLD SITTING AT HOME ALL ALONE WITHOUT A DATE TONIGHT, ANDREA?

WHO CARES?

I CARE.

I WANT TO KNOW HOW BIG A GROUP I'M A PART OF.

YOU CAN'T CHANGE IRVING, CATHY.

I KNOW THAT, ANDREA.

IRVING WILL ALWAYS BE JUST LIKE IRVING IS.

I KNOW.

WELL, IF YOU KNOW YOUR DIFFERENCES ARE IRRECONCILABLE, WHY ARE YOU STILL GOING OUT WITH HIM??

I'M BUYING TIME TILL I FIGURE OUT WHAT ELSE TO DO.

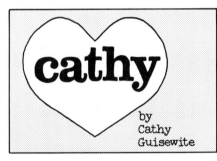

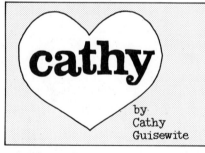

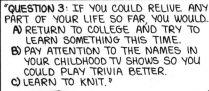

As a last ditch attempt to quit eating several years ago, I started smoking. Unfortunately, the only time I lost any weight was immediately after my first cigarette, which made me throw up.

On one hand, it seemed a little cruel to share this particular vice with Cathy. On the other hand, in light of the number of women whose liberation has included the freedom to start smoking, it seemed very appropriate. Besides, I didn't think it was fair that Cathy should go completely untouched by something that's made me so miserable.

For Cathy and me and millions like us, the hardest part about quitting smoking is a lot like the worst of any diet. It isn't the agony of withdrawal that's so bad. It's the agony of having nothing to do with your mouth.

You build resolve and will power. You arm yourself with statistics and guilt. So at the moment of smashing out that last cigarette, you are a monument of strength and drive, all directed toward the goal of never, ever lighting up again. And then, all of the sudden, there's nothing to do. But wait . . . and wait . . . and wait . . . and wait . . . and wait . . . and wait . . . and, alas, eat. And, even more alas, have a smoke after your snack.

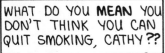

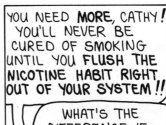

154

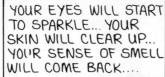

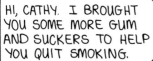

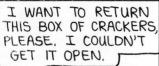

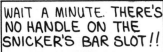

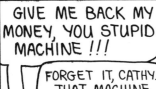

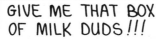

I THOUGHT YOU WERE GOING TO SEE "CLOSE ENCOUNTERS" TONIGHT, CATHY.

I AM... BUT I JUST HAVE TO READ THIS REVIEW OF IT FIRST.

FOR WHAT??

I WANT TO MAKE SURE I HAVE SOMETHING WITTY TO SAY WHEN I WALK OUT OF THE MOVIE.

CAN'T YOU DO THAT ON YOUR OWN?? DON'T YOU HAVE YOUR OWN OPINIONS??!!

OF COURSE I DO, ANDREA.

I'M JUST ALWAYS MORE SURE OF MY OPINIONS IF I'VE READ THEM IN THE NEWSPAPER FIRST.

EXCUSE ME, MISS, BUT I NOTICED THAT THIS ONE BOTTLE OF HAIR CONDITIONER COSTS $7, AND THIS OTHER ONE ONLY COSTS 29¢.

COULD YOU TELL ME WHAT THE BIG DIFFERENCE IS?

CERTAINLY.

THE $7 BOTTLE IS SMALLER.

I'M WEARING AN ACRYLIC SWEATER, POLYESTER SLACKS, SYNTHETIC UNDERWEAR, AND CREPE-SOLED VINYL SOLES.

I'M SITTING ON A FOAM-RUBBER CHAIR, AT A FORMICA TABLE, ON A LINOLEUM FLOOR.

I PAID FOR IT ALL WITH MASTER CHARGE, BANK AMERICARD, AND AMERICAN EXPRESS.

MY PLASTIC HAS JUST REPRODUCED ITSELF.

OOPS. SORRY I'M LATE.

NO YOU'RE NOT, IRVING. THIS ARTICLE SAYS PEOPLE WHO ARE ALWAYS LATE ARE LATE ON PURPOSE

IT'S YOUR LITTLE WAY OF DEFYING THE AUTHORITY FIGURE THAT SAYS YOU HAVE TO BE ON TIME.

BY BEING LATE, YOU'RE JUST SCREAMING TO THE WORLD THAT YOU REFUSE TO LIVE BY OTHER'S TIME STANDARDS!

COME ON, CATHY.. ..LET'S JUST GO.

WE CAN'T. I'M NOT QUITE READY YET.

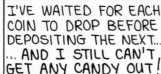

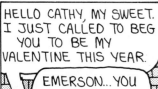

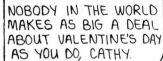

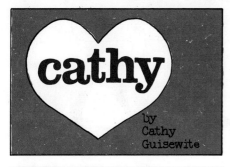

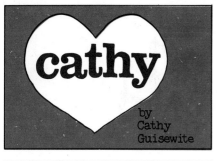

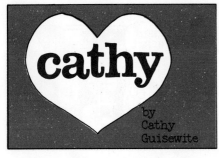

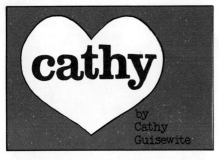

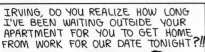

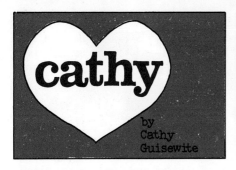

WANT TO FIND ICICLES AND HAVE A SWORD FIGHT WITH THEM?
NO.

WANT TO BUILD A SNOWMAN?
NO.

WANT TO MAKE SNOW ANGELS, IRVING?
NO. THAT'S JUST FOR KIDS.

HOW ABOUT IF I RUN AHEAD, THEN YOU CATCH ME AND WASH MY FACE WITH SNOW?
NO. THAT'S FOR KIDS.

WANT TO SEE WHO CAN SLIDE DOWN THE HILL THE FASTEST WITHOUT SMASHING INTO A TREE??
NO. THAT'S KID'S STUFF, CATHY.
©1977 Universal Press Syndicate

IRVING, DON'T YOU UNDERSTAND **ANYTHING**?!! SOME OF THE MOST SPECIAL MOMENTS YOU CAN HAVE IN A RELATIONSHIP ARE DOING THE THINGS YOU USED TO DO AS KIDS!!!

CATHY, WHAT IS SO SPECIAL ABOUT RUNNING AROUND IN THE SNOW LIKE A 6-YEAR-OLD?!!!

IT HELPS YOU FORGET HOW BORING IT IS TO BE A GROWN UP.
Guisewite 12-11

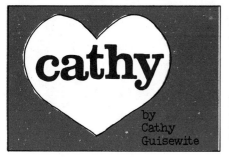

Dear Santa Claus, Sorry I haven't written in so long.....

Dear Santa Claus, Every year I try to write and tell you how good I've been... But every year I get more confused.

My mother says I'm a **good girl** if I start each day with a nourishing breakfast, keep my personal appearance neat, and don't stay out past midnight...

My boyfriend, Irving, says I'm a **good lady** if I pay my own way at the movies and volunteer to do his laundry so he doesn't have to beg me to do it...

My friend Andrea says I'm a **good woman** if I stand up for myself as an intelligent, independent human being and don't pay any attention to what other people expect of me.

How do **I** know if I've been good or not, Santa ??
©1977 Universal Press Syndicate

I can't even figure out which age bracket I fall into.
Guisewite 12-17

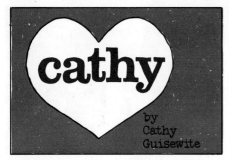

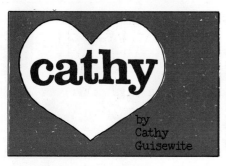

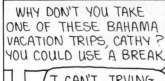

WHAT DO YOU MEAN, YOU THINK YOU'RE CANCELLING YOUR TRIP TO THE BAHAMAS, CATHY?!!

I'M JUST AFRAID OF BEING ALONE, ANDREA.

I'M AFRAID TO FLY ALONE... I'M AFRAID TO EAT ALONE...I'M AFRAID TO WALK THE STREETS ALONE... I'M AFRAID TO GO OUT ALONE...

CATHY, THE ONLY THING YOU'RE REALLY AFRAID OF IS DISCOVERING THAT YOU CAN MAKE IT YOURSELF!! YOU'RE JUST AFRAID OF YOURSELF!!

I NEVER THOUGHT OF THAT, ANDREA.

THAT MAKES ME A COMPLETE COWARD.

DON'T YOU WANT TO KNOW THE NUMBER WHERE I CAN BE REACHED ON MY VACATION, MR. PINKLEY?

NO, CATHY. JUST ENJOY YOURSELF.

DON'T YOU WANT ME TO TYPE OUT A MINUTE-BY-MINUTE INSTRUCTION SHEET FOR THE PERSON WHO'LL BE TAKING MY PLACE??

NO...WE CAN HANDLE IT.

DON'T YOU NEED ME HERE AT ALL, MR. PINKLEY??!!

CATHY, IT'S ONLY A VACATION. WE'LL GET ALONG FINE.

I HATE IT WHEN THE ONLY ONE WHO THINKS I'M INDISPENSABLE IS ME.

YOU'RE TAKING ALL THIS FOR A ONE WEEK TRIP??

YEAH. IF I MEET SOME GUY WHO WANTS TO TAKE ME TO FANCY RESTAURANTS, I'LL NEED ALL MY BEST DRESSES.

IF I MEET SOME GUY WHO LIKES TO SAIL, I'LL HAVE TO HAVE ALL MY BOAT CLOTHES...IF I MEET ...

YOU'RE NOT SUPPOSED TO WORRY ABOUT THAT STUFF WHEN YOU'RE PACKING, CATHY!!!

YOU'RE RIGHT, ANDREA.

I SHOULD WORRY ABOUT MEETING SOME GUY WHO CAN LIFT MY SUITCASES.

DO YOU THINK CATHY WILL BE OKAY BY HERSELF IN THE BAHAMAS?

OF COURSE SHE WILL. CATHY'S A GROWN WOMAN.

SHE LIVES BY HERSELF... ...SHE TAKES CARE OF HERSELF... YOUR DAUGHTER IS NOT A BABY ANYMORE!!!

BYE, MOM AND DAD.

HOWEVER, MY DAUGHTER IS.

EXCUSE ME, MA'AM, BUT YOUR CHILD JUST THREW HIS CHICKEN TETRAZZINI IN MY LAP AGAIN.

OH, HOWARD, YOU LITTLE RASCAL.

UM, EXCUSE ME AGAIN, BUT DO YOU THINK LITTLE HOWARD WILL SCREAM LIKE THAT FOR THE FULL 5 HOUR FLIGHT TO THE BAHAMAS?

OH NO...WE'LL JUST FIND SOMETHING FOR HIM TO DO.

EXCUSE ME ONCE MORE, BUT DO YOU THINK HOWARD COULD DO SOMETHING BESIDES EAT MY CIGARETTES?

CIGARETTES?! YOU CAN'T HAVE CIGARETTES HERE!!

WE NON-SMOKERS HAVE OUR RIGHTS, YOU KNOW!!

I CAN'T GO OUT THERE TO LIE IN THE SUN! ALL THOSE PEOPLE ARE ALREADY THIN AND TAN!

WHAT DO YOU EXPECT? THIS IS THE BAHAMAS.

CHANGING ROOMS

YEAH, BUT THE PEOPLE IN OUR TOUR GROUP AREN'T ALL THIN AND TAN! WHERE'S MY MORAL SUPPORT??

TO POOL

WHERE ARE ALL THE FAT, PALE PEOPLE I CAME HERE WITH ON THE AIRPLANE??!!

RELAX, CATHY. I'M SURE YOUR GROUP WILL BE ALONG SOON.

THERE ARE NEVER ANY FAT, PALE PEOPLE WHEN YOU NEED THEM.

6 FT.

HOW WAS YOUR LUNCH, CATHY? I SEE YOU HAD THE CONCH SHELL SOUP.

JUST FINE, THANKS.

OH GOOD. SO OFTEN WE FIND THAT YOUNG PEOPLE ON OUR BAHAMAS TOURS ARE A LITTLE NERVOUS ABOUT TRYING NEW THINGS.

THEY FIND IT DIFFICULT TO ENJOY EXPERIENCES OTHER THAN THOSE THEY'RE ALREADY FAMILIAR WITH.

OH, NOT ME. I'M READY FOR ANYTHING!!

WONDERFUL! WHAT DID YOU PLAN TO DO THIS AFTERNOON?

EAT DINNER.

I HAVE WANDERED DOWN MILES OF DAZZLING WHITE BEACH, AND NO GORGEOUS MAN WAS SPLASHING ALONG BESIDE ME, HOLDING MY HAND....

I HAVE FELT THE EVENING BREEZE BRUSH MY FACE, AND NO HANDSOME GUY WAS GAZING AT THE REFLECTION OF THE SUNSET IN MY EYES...

I HAVE EXPLORED THE MYSTERIES OF THE CORAL... I HAVE SIPPED THE JUICES OF THE TROPICS, AND NO 6'2" HUNK WAS AT MY SIDE...

I THINK I TAKE MY TRAVEL BROCHURES TOO SERIOUSLY.

DON'T FORGET THE COMPLIMENTARY GOOMBAY COCTAIL PARTY AT THE HOTEL POOL TONIGHT, CATHY.

COMPLIMENTARY?

IS IT COMPLIMENTARY LIKE THE EXTRA $7 WE HAD TO SPEND ON THE SCENIC BOULDER TOUR YESTERDAY ??...LIKE THE $4.50 CHARGE YOU FORGOT TO MENTION FOR OUR NATIVE DANCE CLASS TODAY ???

OH NO. THIS IS COMPLETELY FREE.

OH YEAH? WHAT DO YOU DO THERE ??

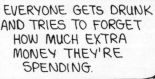
EVERYONE GETS DRUNK AND TRIES TO FORGET HOW MUCH EXTRA MONEY THEY'RE SPENDING.

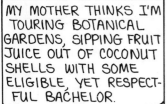
MY MOTHER THINKS I'M TOURING BOTANICAL GARDENS, SIPPING FRUIT JUICE OUT OF COCONUT SHELLS WITH SOME ELIGIBLE, YET RESPECTFUL BACHELOR.

ANDREA THINKS I'M LOUNGING IN THE SUN, DISCUSSING THE E.R.A., WHILE SOME GORGEOUS GUY SMEARS PAPAYA OIL ON MY FEET.

IRVING THINKS I'M HITTING EVERY BAR AND DISCO IN THE BAHAMAS, DANCING AND DRINKING MY BRAINS OUT.

EVERYONE ALWAYS HAS A BETTER TIME ON MY VACATIONS THAN I DO.

WHAT DO YOU MEAN, OUR PLANE LEAVES FOR HOME TOMORROW?! I DON'T HAVE PRESENTS FOR ANYONE YET!

I DON'T HAVE ANY POSTCARDS YET!! I HAVEN'T RECORDED MY MEMORIES WITH PICTURES!! I DON'T EVEN HAVE A SUNTAN!!

YOU'RE NOT SUPPOSED TO WORRY ABOUT THAT STUFF, CATHY. YOU'RE IN THE BAHAMAS TO RELAX.

RELAX? HOW CAN I RELAX??

THIS IS THE ONLY VACATION I'VE GOT !!

WELCOME HOME, CATHY !!

OH ANDREA, I'M GOING TO REMEMBER THAT VACATION FOR THE REST OF MY LIFE !!

OH, BEFORE I FORGET, YOUR BOSS WANTS YOU TO CALL HIM ABOUT SOME EMERGENCY AT WORK...GUESS WHAT? YOUR APARTMENT BUILDING WAS ON THE NEWS BECAUSE ALL THE PIPES BROKE AND....

YOUR MOM WANTS ME TO REMIND YOU THAT YOU PROMISED TO MAKE 300 KLEENEX FLOWERS FOR HER LUNCHEON TOMORROW ....SOME JERK SMASHED YOUR FENDER IN THE PARKING LOT...IRVING SAID THE SECOND YOUR VACATION IS OVER YOU.....

WHAT VACATION?

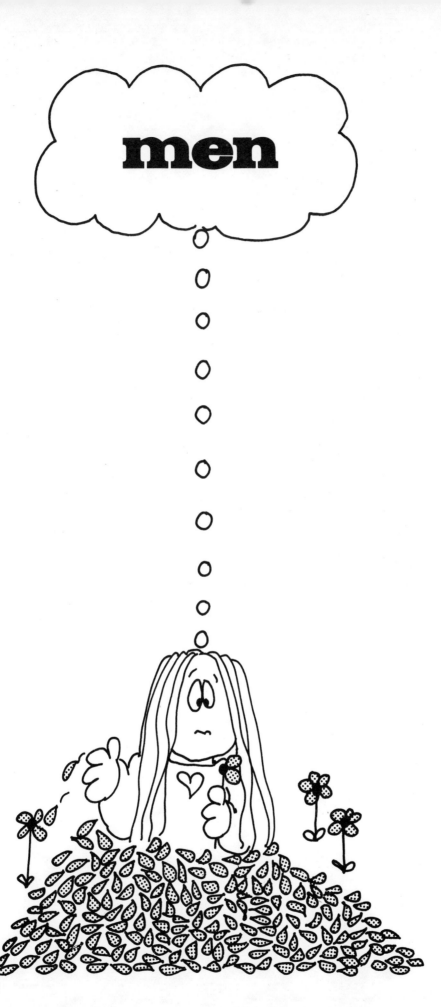

Of all the comments Cathy gets, two of the most common are, "I love the strips about Cathy and Irving. I can really identify with that relationship," and "When is Cathy going to get rid of that jerk?"

The fact that both comments usually come from the same person makes me suspect it's a relationship Cathy isn't exactly living alone. It's a relationship that her brain thinks she should get out of as soon as possible . . . and that her heart can't stand to be without for one second.

175

In no other part of her life is Cathy as confused by what the women's movement has taught her and what her emotions say she needs. It's one thing to take charge of her life in her career, and to stand up for her rights at the department store. But being assertive in a relationship is just not the same as sending a steak back. And the ultimate risk of losing what she has with Irving never seems worth what she might gain on her own.

Even Emerson, who adores her, isn't enough of a lure. And meeting someone new simply isn't as much fun as it's supposed to be.

People who dream of their happy-go-lucky single days forget what work it can be to get someone new to think all your little quirks are cute. People who talk about the excitement of the unknown forget how boring a blind date can be. People who declare that this is the greatest decade in history to be single just don't know the reality of it all: Even Mary Tyler Moore has found something else to do on Saturday night.

MY SECRETARY, ALEX, HAS BEEN COMPLAINING ABOUT NOT BEING ABLE TO COPE WITH THE NEW ATTITUDES OF WOMEN... ...AND IT'S GIVEN ME AN IDEA, ANDREA.

I'M GOING TO START UP A CLASS THAT TEACHES MALE SURVIVAL.

CATHY, THAT'S **BRILLIANT** !!!

BY HELPING MEN LEARN HOW TO ADAPT TO HOW THINGS ARE CHANGING, YOU'LL BE HELPING ALL WOMEN REACH OUR GOAL OF EQUALITY !!!!

NOT TO MENTION MY GOAL OF BEING IN CHARGE OF A ROOMFUL OF GUYS.

THREE OF MY FRIENDS WANT TO JOIN THE MALE SURVIVAL CLASS YOU'RE STARTING, CATHY.

SEE, IRVING? MEN **DO** WANT TO LEARN TO TAKE CARE OF THEMSELVES!

THEY **DO** WANT TO FEEL THE SATISFACTION THAT COMES FROM MAKING THEIR KITCHENS GERM-FREE AND THEIR WASH APRIL FRESH !!

THEY DO WANT TO EXPERIENCE THE SPECIAL POWER A WOMAN HAS IN HER HOME !!!

THEY ALREADY HAVE, CATHY.

ALL THEIR GIRLFRIENDS THREATENED TO DUMP THEM IF THEY DIDN'T SIGN UP.

WELCOME TO MY CLASS ON MALE SURVIVAL. IN THIS FIRST SESSION, WE WILL LEARN TO IDENTIFY COMMON HOUSEHOLD ITEMS.

NOW, JIM, CAN YOU TELL ME WHAT THIS IS?

I THINK IT'S A BROOM.

IRVING??

A SEWING MACHINE??

ALEX???

A TRASH MASHER???

YOU DUMMIES, THIS IS AN IRON !!!

MALE SURVIVAL SEMINAR

5 OR 7 IRON?

MALE SURVIVAL SEMINAR

A CRUCIAL PART OF MALE SURVIVAL IS FOR MEN TO LEARN TO DO THEIR LAUNDRY ALL BY THEM-SELVES.

MALE SURVIVAL SEMINAR

HERE WE HAVE PRE-SOAK, STAIN SPRAY, DETERGENT, BLEACH, FABRIC SOFTENER AND SPRAY STARCH.

MALE SURVIVAL SEMINAR

NOW, ALEX, **WITHOUT THE HELP** OF A GIRLFRIEND, A CLEANING LADY, A SISTER OR A LAUNDRY SERVICE... TELL THE CLASS WHAT YOU WOULD DO FIRST TO GET YOUR LAUNDRY DONE !!

CALL MY MOTHER.

MALE SURVIVAL SEMINAR

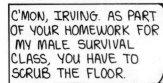

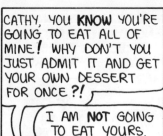

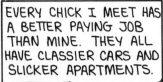

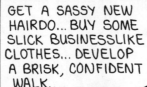

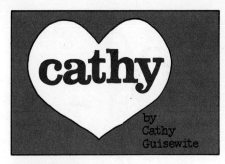

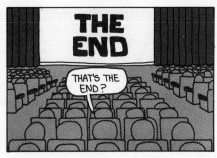

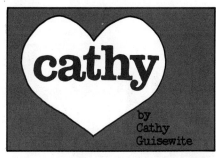

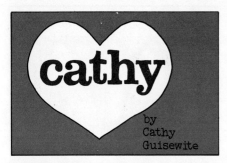

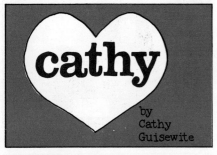

186

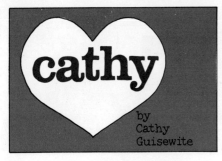

IF IRVING WERE HERE, EVERYTHING WOULD BE WONDERFUL.

IF IRVING AND I WERE WALKING IN THE PARK HOLDING HANDS, EVERYTHING WOULD BE WONDERFUL.

IF IRVING AND I WERE DRINKING HOT CHOCOLATE IN SOME COZY LITTLE CAFE, EVERYTHING WOULD BE WONDERFUL.

IF IRVING AND I WERE SAYING A TENDER, YET LONGING, GOODNIGHT AT MY DOOR, EVERYTHING WOULD BE WONDERFUL.

IF IRVING WERE HERE, EVERYTHING WOULD BE WONDERFUL.

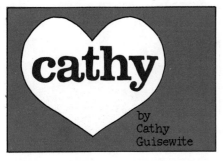

HI. I THOUGHT YOU WERE GOING TO SLEEP IN THIS MORNING.

I COULDN'T. I HAD TOO MUCH ON MY MIND.

WHAT?

I WAS TRYING TO FIGURE OUT WHAT TO DO WHEN I WOKE UP

WHAT ARE YOU GOING TO DO TODAY, CATHY?

I DON'T KNOW, ANDREA. PART OF ME THINKS I SHOULD SPEND THE DAY EXPLORING EXCITING NEW CAREER POSSIBI-LITIES FOR WOMEN....

...AND PART OF ME THINKS IT'S TIME TO CHANGE THE SHELF PAPER.

PART OF ME THINKS I SHOULD READ UP ON HOW WOMEN NO LONGER HAVE TO BE SLAVES TO THEIR HOMES....

...AND PART OF ME THINKS I SHOULD DEVOTE THE DAY TO GETTING MY CLOSETS ORGANIZED.

PART OF ME THINKS I SHOULD BE PRACTICING TECHNIQUES FOR ASSERTIVE BEHAVIOR....

...AND PART OF ME THINKS I SHOULD UNTANGLE THE LOAD OF PANTYHOSE I PUT THROUGH THE DRYER.

HOW'S A WOMAN SUPPOSED TO DO **ANYTHING** ANYMORE, ANDREA ??!

ALL OF THE SUDDEN, WE'VE GOT TOO MANY PARTS!

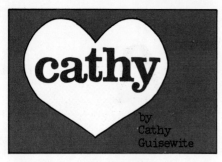

cathy
by Cathy Guisewite

HI, CATHY. I CALLED YOU LAST NIGHT, BUT YOU WEREN'T HOME.

WHY DID YOU CALL?

I WANTED TO SEE IF YOU WERE HOME OR NOT.

ONE OF MY FRIENDS FIXED ME UP WITH A NECKTIE SALESMAN NAMED FRANK LAST NIGHT, MOM.

OH, CATHY, I'D LOVE TO HEAR ABOUT IT.

WELL, FIRST FRANK PICKED ME UP AND TOOK ME TO HOWARD JOHNSON'S FOR A FRIED CLAM DINNER. WE HAD COLE SLAW ON THE SIDE, AND FRANK HAD BUTTER PECAN ICE CREAM FOR DESSERT.

OH, HOW NICE!

THEN WE WENT TO SEE "PETE'S DRAGON". FRANK HAD BOUGHT THE TICKETS AHEAD, IN CASE THERE WAS A BIG LINE-UP AT THE DOOR.

OH, ISN'T THAT SWEET!

AFTER THE MOVIE, FRANK TOOK ME TO THE BIG BOY FOR COFFEE. WE TALKED ABOUT THE NECKTIE BUSINESS FOR AWHILE, CHATTED ABOUT OUR HOPES AND DREAMS FOR THE FUTURE, AND THEN HE TOOK ME HOME.

OH, CATHY, WHAT FUN! IT MUST BE SO WONDERFUL TO BE A YOUNG, SINGLE GIRL!!!

EVERY NOW AND THEN IT'S WORTH IT TO ACTUALLY GO ON A DATE THAT YOU CAN TELL YOUR MOTHER ABOUT.

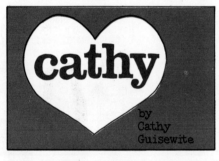

cathy
by Cathy Guisewite

IS IT MY TURN YET?

WELL, LET'S SEE...

OOPS. I'M ALMOST OUT OF CHANGE. DO YOU MIND IF I OPEN UP SOME NEW ROLLS OF NICKELS AND PENNIES BEFORE I RING YOU UP?

WELL, YES, AS A MATTER OF FACT, I DO MIND.

THE LADY IN FRONT OF ME COULD ONLY FIND 5 PIECES OF I.D., SO IT TOOK 20 MINUTES TO CLEAR HER CHECK.

THE LADY IN FRONT OF HER SPENT 15 MINUTES GOING BACK TO THE DAIRY CASE TRYING TO FIND A CARTON THAT DIDN'T HAVE ANY SMASHED EGGS IN IT.

THE LADY IN FRONT OF HER YELLED AT HER TWINS FOR 5 MINUTES EACH FOR DUMPING THAT JAR OF MAPLE SYRUP ON YOUR CONVEYOR BELT.

I'VE ALREADY BEEN WAITING IN LINE FOR 45 MINUTES TO BUY 9 CRUMMY CANS OF TUNA FISH!!!

I'M SORRY, MISS... ...BUT YOU'LL HAVE TO TAKE THOSE TO A DIFFERENT AISLE.

EXPRESS LANE 8 ITEMS OR LESS

THIS IS THE EXPRESS LANE.

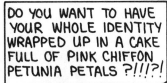

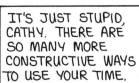

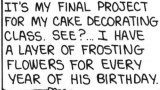

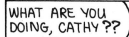

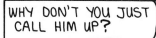

I JUST HAD A GREAT IDEA, ANDREA. I'M GOING TO HAVE A HALLOWEEN PARTY...

...AND INVITE ALL THE MEN I'VE EVER HAD A REAL INTEREST IN SO I CAN MAKE IRVING JEALOUS!!

OH YEAH? WHO'S ON THE LIST?

SO FAR, I'VE GOT DAD AND GRANDPA.

WHAT KIND OF GAMES SHOULD I HAVE AT MY HALLOWEEN PARTY, IRVING?

GAMES?! CATHY, THAT'S FOR KIDS.

WELL, WHAT ARE GROWN-UPS SUPPOSED TO DO AT PARTIES??

THEY'RE SUPPOSED TO STAND AROUND AND GET DRUNK SO THEY WON'T BE BORED.

THAT DOESN'T SOUND LIKE ANY FUN!!

SURE IT IS.

AFTER EVERYBODY GETS DRUNK, THEY START PLAYING GAMES.

WHERE'S YOUR HALLOWEEN CANDY, ANDREA?

I'M GIVING OUT GRANOLA THIS YEAR. IT'S BETTER FOR THE CHILDREN.

ANDREA, KIDS DON'T WANT TO TURN INTO HEALTH FREAKS ON HALLOWEEN! THEY WANT CANDY!!

THINK OF ALL THE DISAPPOINTED LITTLE FACES YOU'LL SEE WHEN YOU HAND OUT THAT STUFF!!

THE KIDS WILL GET PLENTY OF CANDY OTHER PLACES, CATHY.

THEN THINK OF MY DISAPPOINTED LITTLE FACE!!!

CREPE PAPER... APPLES... GOBLIN FACES... FAKE WORMS AND EYEBALLS... WITCHES... SKELETONS.....

I'VE GOT EVERY TRICK IN THE BOOK.

HI, CATHY. IT'S IRVING. SORRY, BUT I CAN'T MAKE IT TO YOUR HALLOWEEN PARTY.

...BUT NO TREAT.

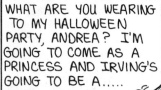

OKAY, IRVING. HOW COME YOU ALWAYS TURN THE LIGHTS OUT WHEN YOU KISS ME ???

GIMME A BREAK, CATHY! I WAS JUST TRYING TO BE A LITTLE ROMANTIC!

I THINK YOU DO IT SO YOU CAN PRETEND I'M SOMEONE ELSE!

DON'T BE SILLY, RUTHANN.

ANDREA, HOW COME YOU'RE ALWAYS SO GORGEOUS AND INTERESTING, AND I'M ALWAYS SO DUMPY AND DULL?

BECAUSE YOU **REPRESS** YOURSELF, CATHY. YOU WORRY SO MUCH ABOUT WHAT OTHER PEOPLE THINK THAT YOU DON'T **LET** YOURSELF BE PRETTY AND BRIGHT!!

BUT WOMEN TODAY DON'T HAVE TO DO THAT ANY-MORE! CATHY, THERE'S A DAZZLING PERSON INSIDE YOU JUST **WAITING** FOR YOU TO SET HER FREE!!!!

I THINK SHE'S TAKING A NAP.

C'MON, CATHY! THE HACKETTS' PARTY HAS BEEN GOING ON FOR 3 HOURS ALREADY!

FASTER, CATHY, FASTER! THE EXERCISE IS GOOD FOR YOU!!

ONLY 4 MORE BLOCKS TO GO!!!

I FAIL TO SEE WHY YOU KEEP REFERRING TO THIS AS "FASHIONABLY" LATE.

HI CATHY. THIS IS EMERSON.

EMERSON??

YEA. REMEMBER ON OUR LAST DATE BACK IN JULY WHEN I ASKED WHEN I COULD SEE YOU AGAIN? YOU LAUGHED AND SAID, "HOW ABOUT SEPTEMBER 29?"...

WELL, THIS IS **IT**!!! THIS IS SEPTEMBER 29!

I HATE IT WHEN THE FUTURE COMES BACK TO HAUNT ME.

If the world belongs to the young, the single, and the free, how come everything comes in packages that serve a family of six? Why do restaurants always stick single people at skimpy little tables in the worst eleven inches of the whole place?

Some of Cathy's best and worst moments are spent trying to get some service from the institutions that serve us.

Even going through assertiveness training hasn't helped. As Cathy's discovered, there just is no satisfaction in speaking your mind to a waitress who's counting the seconds until her next break. All the self-confidence in the world does not make the computer that gobbled up all your money care. Sales clerks either pretend you're not there or lie and say the pink horizontal stripe makes you look like a size five. All of which is made way worse when you sense the secret delight everyone takes in frustrating you.

Not that we shouldn't try to keep some optimism. If nothing else, the institutions that serve us serve to unite us in our aggravation and, in that way, assure us of never being alone. As Cathy might point out, just look at all the friends you have who are mad at the phone company.

202

HELLO. AND WELCOME TO PEOPLE'S BANK AND TRUST. WE'RE PEOPLE WHO CARE ABOUT PEOPLE.

WE'RE FRIENDLY PEOPLE! HONEST PEOPLE!! AND MOST OF ALL, WE'RE PEOPLE PEOPLE!!!

CAN ONE OF YOUR PEOPLE JUST TELL ME HOW MUCH MONEY I HAVE IN MY ACCOUNT?

OH, SORRY, MA'AM. WE CAN'T HELP YOU THERE.

OUR COMPUTER BROKE DOWN.

HI THERE. HOW CAN THE FRIENDLY PEOPLE AT PEOPLE'S BANK AND TRUST HELP YOU NICE PEOPLE TODAY?

WELL, I JUST SPENT THE LAST 12 HOURS GOING OVER EVERY TRANSACTION OF MY LIFE, AND I'D LIKE TO KNOW WHY MY FIGURES SAY I HAVE $233.00 IN MY ACCOUNT, AND YOURS SAY I ONLY HAVE 17¢.

CERTAINLY. THAT'S WHAT THE PEOPLE AT PEOPLE'S ARE HERE FOR.

WELL??

YOU MADE A MISTAKE.

WELCOME ONCE AGAIN TO PEOPLE'S BANK AND TRUST... WHERE PEOPLE MAKE THE DIFFERENCE.

I WOULD LIKE ONE OF YOUR PEOPLE TO MAKE THE DIFFERENCE BE-TWEEN THE $233.00 I SAY I HAVE IN MY ACCOUNT AND THE 17¢ YOU SAY I HAVE!!

OH, WELL, OUR PEOPLE CAN'T MAKE THAT KIND OF DIFFERENCE... WE MAKE THE DIFFERENCE WITH OUR CHEERFUL SERVICE!

WELL, NO WONDER YOU'RE CHEERFUL.

YOU HAVE ALL THE MONEY!!!

HOW DID THINGS WORK OUT AT THE BANK, CATHY?

THEY WON, ANDREA. THE BANK ALWAYS WINS.

WELL, DON'T YOU FEEL BETTER FOR HAVING PUT UP A FIGHT?

NO, ANDREA. I FEEL STUPID. I MADE A BIG FUSS, AND IT TURNED OUT THAT I'D BEEN WRONG ALL ALONG.

EVERYTIME I MAKE A BIG FUSS ABOUT SOMETHING, IT TURNS OUT THAT I WAS WRONG!!!

NO, CATHY. YOU'RE WRONG ABOUT THAT.

205

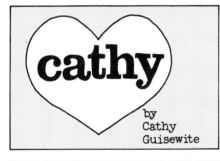

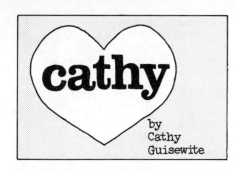

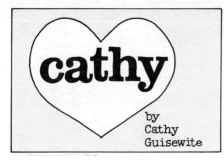

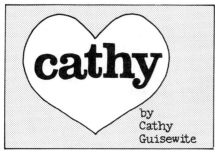

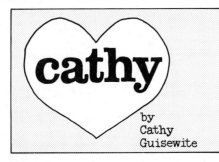

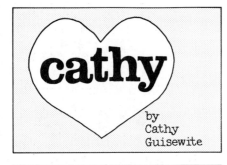

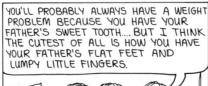

OF COURSE I'M NOT GOING TO QUIZ YOU ABOUT EVERY LITTLE DETAIL OF YOUR DATE LAST NIGHT, CATHY.

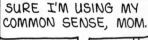

I JUST WANT TO KNOW THAT YOU'RE USING YOUR COMMON SENSE.

SURE I'M USING MY COMMON SENSE, MOM.

I ALSO WANT TO KNOW IF YOUR COMMON SENSE IS STILL THE SAME AS MY COMMON SENSE.

YOU JUST DON'T UNDERSTAND, ANDREA. WHEN IRVING ISN'T HERE, I MISS ALL THE LITTLE THINGS HE DOES FOR ME.

CATHY, IRVING DOESN'T DO **ANYTHING** FOR YOU!!

I MISS ALL THE LITTLE THINGS HE DOESN'T DO.

DEPOSIT $500 IN A NEW ACCOUNT HERE, AND YOU GET YOUR CHOICE OF A FREE ELECTRIC RAZOR OR ALARM CLOCK.

DEPOSIT $5000 AND YOU CAN CHOOSE BETWEEN A FREE PORTABLE MIXER OR ELECTRIC CAN OPENER.

ARE YOU CRAZY??

CERTAINLY NOT. IT'S OUR LITTLE WAY OF ENCOURAGING YOU TO TRUST YOUR MONEY TO US.

WHY WOULD I TRUST MY MONEY TO SOMEONE WHO THINKS THERE'S A $4500 DIFFERENCE BETWEEN AN ALARM CLOCK AND A CAN OPENER?

IF PEOPLE WERE SUPPOSED TO WEAR TOE NAIL POLISH, WE WOULD HAVE BEEN BORN WITH OUR FEET CLOSER TO OUR FACES.

♪ I'M DREAMING OF A POLYESTER CHRISTMAS... ♪

ANDREA, THAT'S **SICK**.

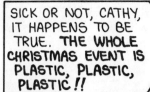

SICK OR NOT, CATHY, IT HAPPENS TO BE TRUE. **THE WHOLE CHRISTMAS EVENT IS PLASTIC, PLASTIC, PLASTIC !!**

I'M NOT PLASTIC, ANDREA... **YOU'RE** NOT PLASTIC.

YOU KNOW...FOR ONCE YOUR OPTIMISM IS MAKING A LITTLE SENSE, CATHY. C'MON.... I'LL HELP YOU GET YOUR NEW CHRISTMAS TREE IN SOME WATER.

FORGET IT, ANDREA.

IT'S PLASTIC.

DID YOU GO CHRISTMAS SHOPPING TODAY, CATHY?

YEAH, MOM. FOR **12 HOURS** !

GOOD GIRL, CATHY ! IT'S REALLY SMART TO JUST PUT IN ONE GOOD SHOPPING DAY AND GET ALL THOSE DECISIONS TAKEN CARE OF **ONCE AND FOR ALL** !!

WHAT DID YOU FINALLY DECIDE ON?

THE WRAPPING PAPER WITH THE LITTLE SNOWMEN ON IT, AND THE MATCHING PINK-STRIPED RIBBON.

YOU'VE BEEN BUYING CHRISTMAS PRESENTS FOR DAD FOR YEARS, MOM. YOU MUST KNOW WHAT I'M GOING THRU TRYING TO FIGURE OUT SOMETHING FOR IRVING.

IT HAS TO BE SOMETHING REALLY **SPECIAL**. IT HAS TO BE **UNIQUE**... **DIFFERENT**...SOMETHING NOBODY ELSE IN THE WORLD WOULD EVER **THINK** TO GIVE HIM !!!

I KNOW JUST WHAT YOU MEAN, CATHY.

OH, MOM...I KNEW YOU'D UNDERSTAND WHY THIS PRESENT HAS TO BE LIKE **NOTHING IRVING'S EVER SEEN BEFORE!**

I FIND YOU NEVER GO WRONG WHEN YOU STICK WITH THE NATIONALLY ADVERTISED BRAND NAMES.

I CAN'T BELIEVE YOU DON'T HAVE IRVING'S CHRISTMAS PRESENT YET, CATHY. YOU'VE BEEN SHOPPING FOR WEEKS !!

I JUST WANT IT TO BE SOMETHING REALLY **SPECIAL**, ANDREA ! I WANT IT TO **MEAN** SOMETHING !!!

CATHY, IF IRVING REALLY CARES ABOUT YOU, ANYTHING YOU GIVE HIM WILL MEAN SOMETHING... WHY **TORTURE** YOURSELF?

I **HAVE** TO, ANDREA.

I CAN NEVER BE SURE SOMETHING WILL MAKE HIM HAPPY UNLESS I MAKE MYSELF MISERABLE ABOUT IT.

YOU'RE LOOKING AT AN ALL NEW EMERSON, CATHY. I HAVE OVERCOME MY FEAR OF REJECTION, AND I'M READY TO GO INTRODUCE MYSELF TO THE LADY OF MY DREAMS.

YOU ARE?

YES, CATHY. IN THE PAST 24 HOURS, I HAVE DEVELOPED NERVE OF STEEL!

I HAVE DEVELOPED A WILL OF IRON!!

WELL, GO GET'EM, EMERSON.

MY TONGUE JUST TURNED TO CEMENT.

LAST WEEK I TOOK A GIRL OUT AND SHE SLAPPED MY FACE BECAUSE I OPENED THE DOOR FOR HER.

THIS WEEK I TOOK ANOTHER GIRL OUT AND SHE SLAPPED MY FACE BECAUSE I DIDN'T OPEN THE DOOR FOR HER.

HOW'S A GUY SUPPOSED TO KNOW HOW TO ACT ANYMORE, CATHY??!

JUST LET THE GIRL YOU'RE WITH KNOW YOU RESPECT HER AS AN EQUAL BY TREATING HER AS AN EQUAL, EMERSON.

WHAT AM I SUPPOSED TO DO, SLAP HER BACK?

LET ME CALL YOU MY SWEETHEART, CATHY.

WELL, YOU CAN CALL ME THAT, EMERSON, BUT THÁT WON'T MAKE ME YOUR SWEETHEART. I'M ALREADY IRVING'S SWEETHEART.

DOES IRVING CALL YOU HIS SWEETHEART?

NO.

IF IRVING DID CALL YOU HIS SWEETHEART, BUT I DIDN'T CALL YOU MY SWEETHEART, WOULD YOU BE MY SWEETHEART?

NO.

LOVE IS TOO COMPLICATED TO DISCUSS BEFORE BREAKFAST.

EMERSON, IT'S OKAY FOR A MAN TO SAY HE'S CONFUSED AND LONELY.

NO IT ISN'T, CATHY. A REAL MÁN IS SUPPOSED TO KEEP HIS FEELINGS INSIDE.

NOT ANYMORE, EMERSON. THE MEN'S LIBERATION MOVEMENT IS SUPPOSED TO FREE MEN FROM THINKING YOU HAVE TO BE UNEMOTIONAL TOWERS OF STRENGTH.

THERE'S A MEN'S LIBERATION MOVEMENT GOING ON?? HOW COME I DIDN'T KNOW THERE WAS A MEN'S LIBERATION MOVEMENT?!!

MAYBE THEY'RE KEEPING IT ALL INSIDE.

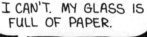

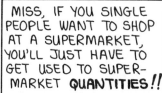

FIRST IRVING SAID HE HATED THE WAY I MUSH UP MY ICE CREAM BEFORE I EAT IT... AND THEN I SAID THAT ANYONE WHO LIKES PINEAPPLE SUNDAES IS STUPID.

THEN IRVING SCREAMED AT ME FOR NOT FIGURING THE TIP OUT IN ONE SECOND, AND I SHOUTED AT HIM FOR WADDING UP HIS NAPKIN ON HIS PLATE.

WAIT A MINUTE, CATHY. THIS DOESN'T SOUND LIKE A VERY SERIOUS FIGHT TO ME.

ARE YOU KIDDING?

THE BIGGER THE FIGHT, THE LITTLER THE THINGS WE YELL AT EACH OTHER ABOUT.

THEY PLAY MUSIC IN THE GROCERY STORE SO YOU'LL BE HAPPY WHILE YOU SPEND ALL YOUR MONEY.

THEY PLAY MUSIC IN THE DENTIST'S OFFICE, SO YOU'LL BE HAPPY WHILE YOUR MOUTH IS BEING DRILLED TO PIECES.

AND NOW THEY PLAY MUSIC OVER THE PHONE, SO YOU'LL BE HAPPY WHILE YOU WAIT FOR 15 MINUTES TO TALK TO SOMEONE.

ALL OF THE SUDDEN, I CAN'T GET MAD WITHOUT HEARING VIOLINS.

NO THANKS, ANDREA. I WANT TO BE BY MYSELF TONIGHT.

NO, I DON'T WANT TO TALK, MOM. I JUST WANT TO BE ALONE.

PLEASE LEAVE ME ALONE TONIGHT, IRVING. I JUST WANT TO BE ALONE.

WAAAH... I DON'T HAVE ANYONE TO TALK TO.

I GOT MY NEW BUDGET WORKED OUT, ANDREA, AND I'M REALLY DETERMINED TO CUT ALL CORNERS THIS TIME.

BRAVO, CATHY!

I THINK I FINALLY DISCOVERED THE ONE THING THAT WILL HELP ME BE A FINANCIALLY INDEPENDENT, COMPLETELY SELF-SUFFICIENT WOMAN!

BRAVO!

I HAVE TO START DATING A GUY WHO'LL PAY FOR MY DINNER.

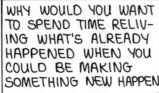

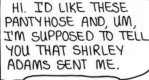

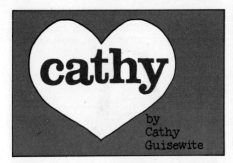

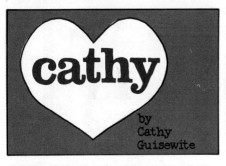

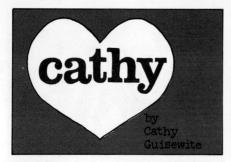

GOOD MORNING LITTLE FLOWER.

GOOD MORNING LITTLE BEE.

HE LOVES ME, HE LOVES ME NOT...

HE LOVES ME, HE LOVES ME NOT...

HE LOVES ME, HE LOVES ME NOT...

HE RESPECTS ME AS AN INDIVIDUAL, HE DOESN'T RESPECT ME AS AN INDIVIDUAL...

HE LOVES ME, HE LOVES ME NOT...

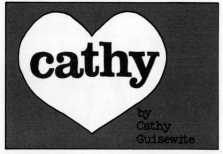

AH, HOME SWEET...

...HOME?

AACK! THIS PLACE IS A MESS!!

DOESN'T ANYBODY BELIEVE IN DOING THE LAUNDRY ANYMORE?!

WHERE'S MY DINNER??

SOMEBODY FORGOT TO TAKE OUT THE GARBAGE AGAIN!!

WHAT AM I SUPPOSED TO DO FOR A CLEAN GLASS?? WASH IT IN THE BATHTUB?!!

THE PROBLEM WITH LIVING BY YOURSELF IS THAT THERE'S NOBODY TO BLAME ANYTHING ON.

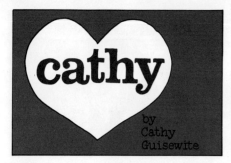

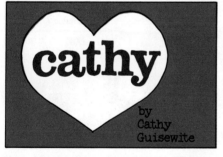

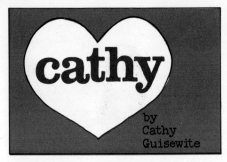

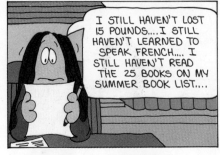

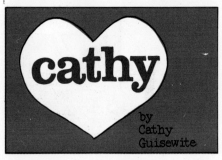